The Satyr of
Titus Petronius Arbiter

THE
satyricon
OF
petronius

The translation by William Burnaby

revised for the present edition, with an

introduction, by Gilbert Bagnani

and illustrated by Antonio Sotomayor

New York

THE HERITAGE PRESS

INTRODUCTION

THERE are many greater works of literature than the *Satyricon* of Petronius but few are more curious, puzzling, and provocative. As we have it to-day, it consists of a number of excerpts, some of considerable length, others of only a few sentences or even words, from the fifteenth and sixteenth books of a long picaresque novel that described the adventures, usually degenerate and repulsive, of an unusually repulsive and degenerate hero-narrator. The plot of the novel, if indeed it had a regular plot, cannot now be recovered, and the purpose of the author seems almost beyond conjecture. It is written in "vulgar" colloquial Latin, a language about which we know next to nothing. The text is corrupt, the interpretation uncertain, the allusions obscure, and even the date and authorship debatable.

As to the date there is now an almost general agreement among scholars that it reflects, accurately and consistently, the life and manners, the social, economic, and even intellectual conditions of Italian provincial towns between A.D. 40 and 70. This being the case it is almost certain that its author was the Petronius who, according to Tacitus, was the Arbiter of Elegance of the court during the earlier part of Nero's reign. "He passed his days in sleep, his nights in business and recreation. He lounged into the fame that others achieve by industry. Yet he was never held to be just a debauched wastrel, like other spendthrifts, but the finished artist in luxury. His words and deeds, the more unconventional and the more careless they appeared to be, were all the more eagerly accepted as evidence of a frank and unsophisticated nature. But as governor of Bithynia and later consul he showed himself a vigorous and able administrator. Then he returned to his vices, real or assumed, and was received by Nero among his few intimates, the Arbiter of Elegance whose sole judgment could determine what pleasures were agreeable and refined." A couple of specimens of his table-talk at this period have been preserved. As a guest recounted with bated breath the nameless orgies of a notorious profligate, Petronius was heard to remark: "What could you expect? I always said the fellow had no imagination!" and at the account of some fantastic extravagance: "Pity he's so terribly stingy!"

As Nero gradually drew the reins of government into his own hands the influence of Petronius declined. Other favourites arose and his great wealth stimulated the greed of a ruler on the verge of bankruptcy. In A.D. 66 Petronius was accused of being indirectly involved in the Pisonian conspiracy of the previous year, and while at Cumae he was informed that his arrest had been ordered. "He would not linger on between hope and fear, but would not take too rapid a farewell of life. He commanded that his veins be opened and then bound up again while talking to his friends on no serious matters nor in the style of one planning a memorable decease. He listened to no disquisitions on the immortality of the soul nor to opinions of philosophers but only to merry songs and light verses. Some of his slaves received his bounty, others the whip. After dining he slept a little that death, though compulsory, might at least seem natural. Even in his will, unlike others, he did not flatter Nero or Tigellinus or any of those in power but wrote out and sealed an account of the Emperor's vices, a list of his male and female paramours and of his innovations in lust, and sent it to Nero. Then he broke his signet ring lest it be used to endanger others." He also broke a valuable glass cup that was coveted by the Emperor.

It is the picture of a man who disguised real abilities and independence under a cloak of languid estheticism, who hated shams, rhetoric, and theatrical gestures, who looked on life steadily and accurately. The *Satyricon* completes Tacitus' sketch. Its author is a realist and a fatalist. We can hear him echoing as he dies the phrases he puts in the mouths of his characters—"You can't take it with you!" as he hurls the precious goblet on the marble floor, or "I have lived in style and I will die in style; what have I to gripe about?" Totally unconcerned with the future or the mysteries of the universe, he is a rationalist with his feet set firmly on the ground. The rites of the old state religion are comic, the popular mystery religions a mere outlet for wealthy nymphomaniacs. Blessed is he who has never had to listen to the windy discussions of philosophers, while astrologers and soothsayers are cheats and charlatans. He tells admirably a couple of excellent ghost stories, invaluable documents for the historian of folklore, but only the vulgar believe such tales. Morality is but an opinion, virtue is unrewarded, and crime certainly pays. The injured man perishes in the storm, the degenerate criminal who injured him is saved.

Almost alone among ancient writers he shows a keen interest in the visual arts, and his opinions on literature are remarkable when we consider how he himself writes. In both art and literature he is an uncompromising conservative, possibly because at that time the ancients were out of fashion and under no circumstances would he follow the crowd. He clearly disliked the rococo style of decoration that was to triumph in Nero's Golden House. He would have considered silly and unreasonable the charming paintings in the house of the Vettii at Pompeii but would probably have approved of those from the Villa at Boscoreale now in the Metropolitan Museum. In Latin his heroes are Cicero, Virgil, Horace, authors at that time out of fashion with the intellectual proletariat that gathered round Seneca, the minister and tutor of Nero and expounder of popular systems of philosophy and ethics for the benefit of cultured millionaires.

For this fashionable clique, for this mutual admiration society,

Petronius feels nothing but contempt. I suspect that certain traits of Trimalchio, his claims to omniscience, his illiterate passion for the humanities, his commonplace philosophizing, his ineffective humanitarianism, may be covert digs at Seneca. An uncompromising realist, he hates the clichés, the rhetoric, the hypocrisy, the self-deception of the possessor of three hundred millions who extols the virtues of poverty, abstinence, and the simple life, of the owner of thousands of slaves who goes on preaching that they are "our brothers under the skin."

The extraordinarily vivid picture of the Oriental freedmen may derive from the direct observation of his own family freedmen, some of whom we know were living at Herculaneum. Perhaps, like Trimalchio's noble friend Scaurus, when he went to Puteoli he preferred to stay with some family Trimalchio and observe his vagaries with an amused eye rather than at "his father's mansion by the sea." And as an accurate and dispassionate observer he has few equals and no superior. He describes with almost clinical accuracy the various stages of intoxication—jocose, grandiose, bellicose, lachrymose, comatose. He notices how the conversation of the illiterate is just a series of commonplaces, proverbial expressions, and trite metaphors and similes. He has an unerring eye for the significant detail: the group in the corner of the forum waving in the twilight the embroidered hem of the stolen robe, the thieves who on discovery pretend to fall down in a drunken stupor, the old gentleman playing at ball in bedroom slippers, the running footmen in their pompous liveries, the old woman on uneven pattens egging on the mastiff, the nail that comes out of the wall with the pot it supports, the poetaster who goes on scribbling during a shipwreck.

He is also remarkable as a psychologist. The palace that Trimalchio is so proud of is an old-fashioned one, the wish-fulfilment of the boy who as a slave lived in such a mansion fifty years earlier. Eighteen centuries before Krafft-Ebing he has identified masochism and sadism. The studies of the masochist degenerate and weakling who is the narrator; of the brutal but vigorous Ascyltos, the perfect foil to such a character; of the transvestite boy, always careful to side with the stronger—are all acute and penetrating. Equally acute and penetrating are his studies of women: Quartilla, the wealthy lady who combines erotic mysticism and sadistic nymphomania, in the seventeenth century would have celebrated the black mass; Circe has *la nostalgie de la boue;* Tryphaena runs after boys; the matron of Ephesus is just pure and simple bitch; Fortunata is the careful housewife who rules her husband and household with a rod of iron painted to look like lath; the vulgar and purse-proud Scintilla is just the sort of woman to attract a vulgar and purse-proud stonemason.

If the purpose of satire is to emend the manners and customs of humanity or denounce its follies and crimes, Petronius is no satirist. There is no trace of Horace's polite smile, of Juvenal's savage indignation, of Swift's dark misanthropy, or even of Addison's supercilious sneer. We hear perhaps a distant echo of elfin laughter—"What fools these mortals be!" Like the *voyous* he so accurately depicts he would appear to be looking at the human comedy through the keyhole of a very solid and well-bolted door. If the scenes so observed are hardly edifying they are certainly strange and amusing, but anyone who suggested that he open the door and take sides in the fray would, like Giton, get his ears well boxed. It is a mistake to consider the work a satire on high society or even "café society" in Rome. It is not "Life in Rome" but "Life in the Provinces"; not high society but low, very low, life. Trimalchio with his thirty millions can cut quite a figure in a country town but he is careful to avoid Rome, where he would be barely rich enough to get elected to a club where fortunes of three hundred millions were not uncommon. He lives in an old-fashioned house with old-fashioned decoration, his bath is hopelessly inelegant, and the splendours that so amaze down-at-heel adventurers are stale, cheap stunts. Petronius smiles impartially at the pride of the parvenu and the admiration of the adventurer.

Yet is his detachment as complete as it seems? Is his purpose only that of entertaining a highly sophisticated court with amusing scenes of low life? The only subject that seems to move Petronius out of his detachment is the crass materialism of the time, "the worship of the almighty Dollar." The very Senate that should set an example thinks Jupiter can be bribed with gold; all fall on their knees to count their money. The easiest way of getting rich quick is to discover a hidden treasure, but all other ways are justifiable. Prostitute your children to get a legacy, embezzle from the estate of which you are executor, bob for pennies in a dung-hill, obey Sir Epicure Mammon's command: "Be rich!" It is this love of money that has caused the decline of literature, rhetoric, the fine arts. Education has been perverted to utilitarian ends. Parents send their little hopefuls to school to fit them for a good job. A "college education" will keep the wolf from the door. "If he doesn't take to the humanities, I'll see he learns a trade, a barber maybe, or a salesman. And if the worst comes to the worst he can always be an attorney!" Such an education corrupts still further the natural depravity of man.

The contrast between the educated and the uneducated is all in favour of the latter. Fortunata and Scintilla, ridiculous, purse-proud, horribly vulgar, are at least genuine persons with a better justification for their existence than the society perverts, Quartilla and Tryphaena. Chrysis the slave is at least normal, her mistress Circe is not. The half-literate Oriental freedmen are vulgar boors but they are not as utterly contemptible as the three delinquent and degenerate students, the toad-eating professor of rhetoric, or that lecherous old goat, the poetaster Eumolpus. The freedman's iron ring will command more credit on 'change than the knight's gold one. Trimalchio, for all his vulgarity and absurdity, is infinitely better than the people who surround him. There is something almost lovable in his longing for love and admiration, in his naïve delight in the applause of his guests, whom he constantly insults through sheer inadvertence.

If there is little to choose between the illiterate and the educated, there is perhaps even less to choose between the vulgar and the elegant. Petronius, in depicting accurately and in detail "low life," may perhaps be holding up a mirror to "high life." Are the vulgarians and adventurers whose activities he describes so amusingly and accurately very different from the sophisticated and elegant members of the imperial court? The calm and fastidious Arbiter of Elegance passes on the whole of humanity the same verdict as Sadie Thompson, the angry prostitute. All men, from Nero in his Golden House to the slave in his garret, all men are alike: "Pigs!"

GILBERT BAGNANI

University of Toronto
Toronto, Ontario

A NOTE ON THE TEXT

THE history of the text is almost as curious as the work itself. At the beginning of the fifth century Sidonius Apollinaris in the South of France had a copy of the *Satyricon* more complete than anything we have to-day. It is probable that this codex was later broken up and many if not most of its sheets were lost. A group of sheets, representing about a third of our present text, including most of the verse, was copied as early as the beginning of the ninth century. In the twelfth century, when there was a revival of interest in Petronius, further sheets were discovered, united to the first group, and copied. From two of these copies, now lost, Jean de Tournes of Lyons in 1575 and Mamert Patisson of Paris in 1577 printed new editions that practically doubled the amount of text known, but only small portions of the "Dinner of Trimalchio" were preserved. Nearly a hundred years later a certain Marino Statileo discovered in a library on the island of Traù (Trogir) in Dalmatia a codex now in Paris that contained the entire "Dinner" copied in 1424 from another codex, also lost, that Poggio Braccio-lini had discovered in England. Its publication caused an immediate storm: at first many scholars denounced it as an obvious and impudent forgery, but its genuineness was soon established beyond all question.

In 1688 "an Austrian army awfully arrayed boldly by battery besieged Belgrade" and eventually took it. In October 1690 a certain François Nodot, at that time serving as commissary to the French armies on the Rhine, wrote to Charpentier, the venerable president of the French Academy—he had been appointed by Colbert—informing him that a friend of his at the sack of Belgrade had discovered a complete manuscript of the *Satyricon* that filled up the still numerous gaps in the story. He had had it transcribed and begged Charpentier to present it to the Academy for its approval and possibly obtain a subvention for the expenses involved in publication. The old man swallowed the bait—hook, line, and sinker—and answered most enthusiastically together with a number of his friends. The edition appeared in 1691, and five more, one bearing the imprint of A. and J. Churchill in London, the following year. In 1694 he gave to the world his own translation. This popularity was his downfall; he was apparently a good commissary—he has to his credit a large and perfectly serious treatise on how to supply armies in the field—but his Latin scholarship was very indifferent. Scholars all over Europe, including Bentley, had no difficulty in proving that the new parts were forgeries and not very skilful forgeries at that. Since, however, they rendered the reading of the text much easier for persons who had little interest in antiquity but a good deal in spicy details they continued to be reprinted to our own day. In the present edition Nodot's forgeries are set off by «French quotation marks.»

In 1694 Nodot's text was "made English by Mr. Burnaby of the Middle Temple and another hand" and "printed for Samuel Briscoe, at the corner of Charles Street, in Russell Street, Covent Garden." The translation is divided into two parts, the first part ending with the Dinner. Burnaby claimed as his own all the verse translations and the second part; the first part was the work of the "other hand," probably a Mr. Wilson, also of the Middle Temple. He dedicates the work to Henry Sidney, Earl of Romney, considered the handsomest man of the time, and in his preface carefully avoids expressing any opinion on the authenticity of the Belgrade fragments, though he translates them. The scholarship of both translators was extraordinarily defective—Burnaby from 1691 to 1693 had been at Merton College, Oxford, and his associate and fellow Templar must also have been a University graduate—but their English had all the lusty vigour of the Restoration. Indeed it was quite frankly salacious, and they delighted in turning the slightest hint or innuendo into downright Anglo-Saxon bawdry. Burnaby himself notes that "fine gentlemen" may "protest I've yet debauched Petronius and robbed him of his language, his only purity." He had indeed!

In 1708 the same printer issued a new version by several eminent hands—Mr. Wilson, Mr. Burnaby, Mr. Thos. Brown, Capt. Ayloff, and several others—which went through numerous editions in the following twenty years. It is in no way a new translation but simply an extensive revision of the earlier one. The original translators and a group of "fine gentlemen," a kind of Covent Garden Scriblerus Club, determined to make Petronius talk the language of a man-about-town, not that of a country bumpkin. Most of the work, I believe, was done by the original translators; the others supplied hints and suggestions and new versions of the shorter poems. They were not in the least concerned with scholarship—they perpetuate most of their original howlers which they could have corrected from the French version, and for good measure add a few new ones—their concern was with style and vocabulary. They removed or toned down most of the verbal smut and carefully changed as far as possible all references to homosexuality, to the point of turning the Pergamene boy into a girl. It was evidently no longer safe under Queen Anne to allude to subjects that could be mentioned with impunity under William of Orange, whose alleged tastes were the subject of universal gossip. They altered all forms of expression that smacked of archaic or rustic diction; "you" is almost everywhere substituted for "thee" and "ye," and "said" for "quoth." The vocabulary is brought up to date: "smell-feasts" is replaced by "parasites," "garbling of peas" by "cleansing of peas," and so forth, marking the change from the English of

Pepys and Bunyan to that of Addison and Swift. In the great majority of cases the changes conform to present-day usage, though the modern reader might find a "scaramouche" even more puzzling than a "merry-andrew." They tightened up, not usually for the better, the loose colloquial syntax, and forced the at times very slipshod clauses into the strait-jacket of conventional grammar. They sought, often felicitously, for modern equivalents for the many commonplaces, proverbial expressions, and similes. Burnaby had translated the verse flatly but on the whole not too unfaithfully: the "hands" replace the shorter poems by "Imitations," loose paraphrases replete with contemporary allusions. This could not be done for the two longer poems that Burnaby had translated in heroic couplets abounding in triple rhymes; moreover, many verses did not scan and still more did not rhyme. He attempted to make these conform more closely to Dryden's example, but the improvement of the prosody was at the expense of both sense and accuracy.

The real merit of these "Augustan" translators, however deficient their Latin scholarship, is that these briefless barristers, half-pay Captains, Grub Street Scribblers, University graduates forced in London to live by their wits, these models for the Vainloves and Mirabells of Congreve, were the last true descendants of Encolpius and Ascyltos. They too lived by pimping, cadging, false pretences, and theft, but, like them, were gaily, not sordidly, immoral. In republishing their work the present editor has arbitrarily selected from the readings of the 1694 and 1708 editions those that seem to him the most felicitous or most easily understood by the modern reader. Wherever possible he has tried to correct the innumerable mistranslations and bring the version closer to the modern critical text; but where this would have involved the rewriting of a long passage, the "pretty Gentlemen" of Queen Anne's day have been allowed to speak their own language. If the present translation is not the exact reproduction of any previous one, it is still by "a number of hands," including the editor's.   G. B.

The Satyr of
Titus Petronius Arbiter

With its Fragments, recover'd at Buda, 1688

Henry Earl of Romney,
Viscount Sidney

Master-General of Their Majesties Ordinance, one of Their Majesties most Honourable Privy-Council, Constable of Dover-Castle, and Lord Warder of the Cinque-Ports.

My LORD,

GOOD Men think the meanest Friend no more to be dispis'd, than the Politick the meanest Enemy; and the Generous wou'd be as inquisitive to discover an unknown Esteem for 'em, as the Cautious an unknown Hatred: This I say to plead my self into the number of those you know for your Admirers; and that the World may know it, give me leave to Present you with a Translation of *Petronius,* and to absolve all my Offences against him, by introducing him into so agreeable Company. You're happy, my Lord, in the most Elegant part of his Character, in the Gallantry and Wit of a Polite Gentleman, mixt with the Observation and Conduct of a Man of Publick Employments; And since all share the benefit of you, 'tis the Duty of all to confess their sence of it, I had almost said, to return, as they cou'd, the Favour, and like a true Author, made that my Gratitude which may prove your Trouble: But what flatters me most out of the apprehensions of your Dislike, is the Gentleman-like Pleasantry of the Work, where you meet with variety of Ridicule on the Subject of *Nero*'s Court,

an agreeable Air of Humour in a Ramble through Schools, Bag-
nio's, Temples, and Markets; Wit and Gallantry in Amours, with
Moral Reflections on almost every Accident of Humane Life. In
short, my Lord, I shall be very proud to Please a *Sidney,* an House
Fertile, of extraordinary Genio's, whose every Member deserves
his own Sir *Philip* to Celebrate him; whose Characters are Ro-
mances to the rest of Mankind, but real Life in his own Family.

> *I am, my Lord,*
> *Your Lordships most devoted*
> *Humble Servant,*

W. BURNABY

The Preface

THE *Moors* ('tis said) us'd to cast their newborn Children into the Sea, and only if they Swam would think 'em worth their Care; but mine, with more neglect, I turn into the World; for sink or swim, I have done all I design'd for't. I have already, with as much satisfaction as *Aeneas* in a Cloud heard *Dido* praise him, heard the *Beaux-Criticks* condemn this Translation before they saw it, and with as much Judgment as if they had: And after they had Prophetically discover'd all the Flaws in the turns of Thought, the cadence of Periods, and had almost brought in *Epick* and *Drama,* they supt their Coffee, took Snuff, and charitably concluded to send *Briscoe* the Pye-Woman to help off with his Books. Well, I have nothing to say, but that these brisk Gentlemen that draw without occasion, must put up without satisfaction.

After the Injury of 1700 Years, or better, and the several Editions in *Quarto, Octavo, Duodecimo,* etc., with their respective Notes to little purpose; for these Annotators upon matters of no difficulty, are so tedious, that you can't get rid of their enlargements without sleeping, but at any real Knot are too Modest to interrupt any Man's Curiosity in the untying of it. After so many Years, I say, it happened upon the taking of *Belgrade* this Author was *made* entire; made so because the New is suspected to be Illegitimate: But it has so many Features of the lawful Father, that he was at least thought of when 'twas got. Now the Story's made out, the character of *Lycas* alter'd, and *Petronius* freed from the imputation of not making Divine or Humane Justice pursue an ill-spent Life.

As to the Translation, the other Hand, I believe, has been very careful; but if my part don't satisfie the World, I should be glad to see my self reveng'd in a better Version; and tho' it may prove no difficult Province to improve what I have done, I shall yet have the credit of the first Attempt.

If any of the Fine Gentlemen should be angry after they have read it, as some, to save that trouble, have before; and protest I've yet debaucht *Petronius,* and robb'd him of his Language, his only Purity, I hope we shall shortly be reconciled, for I have some very pretty new Songs ready for the Press: If this satisfies them, I'll venture to tell others that I have drest the meaning of the Original as modestly as I could, but to have quite hid the obscænity, I thought, were to Invent, not Translate.

As for the Ladies, if any too-discerning antiquated Hypocrite (for only such I fear) shou'd be angry with the beastly Author; let the Work be my Advocate, where the little liberties I take, as modestly betray a broad Meaning, as blushing when a Man tells the Story.

Those who object, that things of this nature ought not to be Translated, must arraign the Versions of *Juvenal, Suetonius,* etc., but what *Suetonius* thought excusable in *History*, any sober Man will think much more allowable in *Satyr:* Nor can this be offensive to Good-manners, since the gross part here is the displaying of Vices of that Dye, that there's an abhorrence even in Nature from 'em; nor is it possible that any ill Man can talk a good one into a new Frame or Composition; nay, perhaps it may be applicable to a good use, to see our own happiness, that we know that to be opposite to Humanity it self, which some of the ancients were deluded even to practise as Wit and Gallantry; thus I'm so far from being toucht in expressing those Crimes, that I think it makes the more for me, the more they're detested.

If I have alter'd or added to the Author, it was either to render those customs of the *Romans* that were analogous to ours, by what was more familiar to us, or to prevent a Note by enlarging on others where I found 'em.

The Verse of both Parts are Mine, and I have taken a great liberty in 'em; and tho' I believe there I have not wrong'd the Original, yet all will not amount to call them *Good*.

The Money at first I made *English* Coin, but not the exact worth, because it would have been odd in some places to have brought in pence and farthings; as when the thousand Sesterces are offered to discover *Gito*, it would not be consistent with the haste they were in to offer so many Pounds, so many Shillings, and so many Pence: I therefore proportioned a summ to the Story without casting up the Sesterces; thus they went to the Press: But advis'd either to give the just value or the *Roman* Coin, I resolv'd on the latter for the Reasons I have given, and alter'd the Summs as the Proofs came to my hands; but trusting the care of one Sheet to a Friend, the summ of 2000 Crowns past unalter'd.   W. B.

THE
First Part
OF THE WORKS OF
Petronius Arbiter
IN PROSE AND
VERSE

MADE ENGLISH BY MR. WILSON OF THE
MIDDLE TEMPLE, AND SEVERAL OTHERS

«"I PROMISED YOU AN account of what befel me and am now resolved to be as good as my word, being opportunely met not only to improve our learning but to be merry and put life into our discourse with pleasanter tales. Fabricius Veiento has already, and that wittily, exposed the juggle of religion and withal discovered with what impudence and ignorance priests pretend to be inspired.»

"But are not our wrangling pleaders possessed with the same frenzy who cant it: 'These wounds I received in defence of your liberty! This eye was lost in your service! Give me a hand to lead me to my children for my severed hams are too feeble to support me!'? Yet even this might pass for tolerable did it put young beginners in the least way to well-speaking. Whereas now, what with the inordinate swelling of matter and the empty rattling of words, they only gain this, that when they come to appear in public they think themselves in another world. And therefore I look upon the young fry of collegiates as likely to make the most promising

3

blockheads, because they neither hear nor see anything that is in use amongst men; but a company of pirates with chains on the shore, tyrants issuing proclamations to make children kill their fathers, the answers of oracles in a plague time that three or more virgins be sacrificed to appease the angry Gods, dainty fine honey-pellets of words without any substance, like a dish prettily garnished without any meat in it, and everything so done as if 'twere all spice and garnish.

"Such as are thus bred can no more judge aright than those that live in a kitchen not stink of the grease. Give me, with your favour, leave to say 'twas you first lost the good grace of speaking; for with light idle jingles of words to make sport you have brought it to this, that the substance of oratory is become effeminate and sunk. Our youth were not confined to this way of declaiming when Sophocles and Euripides influenced the age. Nor yet had any garret-professor debauched their studies when Pindar and the nine lyric poets durst not attempt the inimitable numbers of Homer. And that I may not derive my authority from poets only, 'tis certain neither Plato nor Demosthenes ever put in practice these affected declamations. A stile one would value and, as I may call it, a chaste oration, is not splatchy nor swollen, but rises with a natural beauty. This windy and irregular way of babbling came lately out of Asia into Athens and, having like some ill planet blasted the aspiring genius of their youth, at once corrupted and put a period to all true eloquence. After this, who came up to the height of Thucydides? Who reached the fame of Hyperides? Nay, there was hardly a verse of a right strain, but all, as of the same batch, died with their author. Painting also had the same fate after the boldness of the Egyptians ventured to bring so great an art into miniature."

«At this and the like rate I was upon a time declaiming when one» Agamemnon «made up to us, and looking sharply on a person whom the mob with such diligence gave attention to, he» would not suffer me to declaim longer in the portico than he had sweated in the school but "Young man," said he, "because your discourse is beyond the common apprehension and, which is not often seen, that you are a lover of understanding, I won't deceive you. The masters of these schools are not to blame who think it necessary to be mad with madmen. For unless they teach what their scholars approve, they might, as Cicero says, keep school to themselves. Like flattering parasites who, when they come to great men's tables, study nothing more than what they think may be most agreeable to the company—being sensible they shall never effect their designs unless they first charm the ear—so a master of eloquence, fisherman-like, unless he first baits his hook with what he knows the fish will bite at, may wait long enough on his rock without hopes of catching anything.

"Where lies the fault then? Parents ought to be sharply reprehended who are unwilling their children should observe a strict method in their studies. But in this, as in all things else, they are so fond of making a noise in the world and in such haste to arrive at their wishes that they hurry them into the public ere they have well digested what they have read, and put children, before they are well past their sucking-bottle, into the lists of eloquence, than which even themselves confess nothing is greater. Whereas if they would suffer them to come up by degrees, that their studies might be tempered with grave lectures, their affections fashioned by the dictates of wisdom, that they might work themselves into a mastery of words, and for a long time hear what they're inclined to imitate, nothing that pleased children would be admired by them. But now boys trifle in the schools, young men are laughed at in public, and, which is worse than both, what ill habits are foolishly assumed in youth we refuse to acknowledge in age. But that I may not be thought to condemn Lucilius, as written in haste, I will also myself give you my thoughts in verse.

> Whoe'er would with ambitious just desire
> To mastery in so fine an art aspire
> Must all extremes first diligently shun
> And in a settled course of virtue run.
> Let him not Fortune with stiff greatness climb
> Nor, courtier like, with cringes undermine,
> Nor all the brother blockheads of the pot
> Ever persuade him to become a sot,
> Nor flatter poets to acquire the fame
> Of, I protest, 'a pretty gentleman'!
> But whether in the wars he would be great
> Or in the gentler arts that rule a state

Or else his am'rous breast he would improve,
Well to receive the youthful cares of love,
In his first years, to poetry inclined,
Let Homer's spring bedew his fruitful mind.
His manlier years to manlier studies brought,
Philosophy must next employ his thought;
Then let his boundless soul new glories fire,
And to the great Demosthenes aspire.
When round in throngs the list'ning people come
T'admire what sprung in Greece so slow at home
Raised to this height, your leisure hours engage
In something just and worthy of the stage:
Your choice of words from Cicero derive,
And in your poems you design should live
The joys of feasts and terrors of a war.
More pleasing those, and these more frightful are,
When told by you, than in their acting were.
And thus, enriched with such a golden store,
You're truly fit to be an orator."

While I was wholly taken up with Agamemnon, I did
not observe how Ascyltos had given me the slip, and as
I continued my diligence, a great crowd of scholars
filled the portico, just come from an extemporary decla-
mation of I know not whom, that was descanting on
what Agamemnon had just said. While therefore they
ridiculed his advice and condemned the method of the
whole, I took an opportunity of getting from them and
ran in quest of Ascyltos. But the hurry I was in, with my
ignorance where our inn lay, so distracted me that what
way soever I went I returned by the same; till, tired in
the pursuit and all in a sweat, I met an old herb-woman

and "I beseech you, Mother," says I, "do you know whereabouts I dwell?" Pleased with the simplicity of such a home-bred jest, "Why should I not?" answered she, and getting on her feet went on before me. I thought her no less than a witch. But, having led me into a bye lane, she raised a piebald patched hanging and "Here," says she, "you can't want a lodging."

As I was denying I knew the house, I observed a company of Beaux reading the bills over the cells on which was inscribed the name of the respective whore and her price, and others of the same function, naked, scuttling it here and there as if they would not, yet would be, seen. When too late I found myself in a bawdy-house, cursing the hag that had trapaned me thither, I covered my head and was just making off through the midst of

them, when in the very entry Ascyltos met me, but as
tired as myself and in a manner dead; you'd have sworn
the same old woman decoyed him there. I could not for-
bear laughing, but having saluted each other, I asked
what business he had in so scandalous a place. He wiped
his face and "If you knew," replied he, "what has hap-
pened to me. . . ." "As what?" says I.

He faintly replied: "When I had roved the whole city
without finding where I had left the inn, an old gentle-
man came up to me and kindly proffered to be my
guide. So through many a cross lane and blind turning
having brought me to this house, he drew upon me and
pressed to a closer engagement. In this affliction the
whore of the cell also demanded garnish-money, and
that loose fellow laid such violent hands on me that, had
I not been too strong for him, I had got the worst of it."

«While Ascyltos was telling his tale, in come the same
fellow with a woman, none of the least agreeable, and,
looking upon Ascyltos, entreated him to walk in and
fear nothing, for if he would not be passive he might be
active. The woman on the other hand pressed me to go
in with her. We followed therefore, and being led
among those little apartments we saw many of both
sexes at work,» so that we concluded all of them had
drunk a love potion.

«We were no sooner discovered than they would
have been at us with the like impudence, and in a trice,
one of them, his coat tucked under his girdle, laid hold
on Ascyltos and, having thrown him across a couch,

would have charged him in the rear. I presently ran to help the undermost and» uniting our forces we made nothing of the troublesome fool. «Ascyltos went off and flying left me exposed to their fury, but thanks to my strength I got off without hurt.»

«I had almost traversed the city round when» in the dusk of the evening I saw Gito at the bench of our inn. I placed myself by him «and, going in,» asked him what Ascyltos had got us for dinner. The boy, sitting down on the bed, began to squeeze out the tears from his eyes. I was much concerned at it, and asked him the occasion. He was slow in his answer and unwilling to inform me, but, mixing threats with my entreaties, " 'Twas that brother or comrogue of yours," said he, "that coming

erewhile into our lodging would have violated my virtue. When I cried out, he drew his sword, and 'if thou art a Lucrece,' said he, 'thou hast met a Tarquin!'"

I heard him, and shaking my fist at Ascyltos: "What sayst thou," said I, "thou catamite, whose very breath is tainted?" Ascyltos at first pretended to be mightily surprised, but presently, putting his own fists up, in a still higher voice cried out: "Must you be prating, thou lascivious cut-throat, whom, «condemned for murdering thine host,» nothing but the fall of the scaffold could have saved? You make a noise, you night-pad, who when at thy best hadst never to do with any woman but a bawd! On what account, think you, was I the same to you in the summer house, that the boy here now is?"

"And who but you," interrupted I, "gave me that slip in the portico?" "Why what, my man of Gotham," continued he, "must I have done, when I was dying for hunger? Hear sentences, forsooth, that is, the rattling of broken glasses and the expounding of dreams? So help me Hercules, thou wert by much the greater rogue of the two, who to get a meal's meat did not blush to commend an insipid rhimer!" When at last, turning from scolding to laughing, we began to be in a better humour and to talk of our affairs more soberly.

But the late injury still sticking in my stomach, "Ascyltos," said I, "I find we shall never agree together; therefore let's divide the common stock, and each of us set up for himself. You are a piece of a scholar and so am I. I'll be no hindrance to your projects, but think of some other way, for otherwise we shall run into a thousand mischiefs and become town-talk."

Ascyltos was not against it, and "Since we have promised," said he, "as scholars to sup together, let's husband the night too; and to-morrow I'll get me a new lodging and some comrade or other."

" 'Tis irksome," said I, "to defer what we like." The itch of the flesh occasioned this hasty parting, tho' I had been a long time willing to shake off so troublesome an observer of my actions, that I might renew my old intrigue with my Gito.

«Ascyltos taking the affront, impatiently, without answering, flew away in a fury. I was too well acquainted with his subtle nature and the violence of his love not to fear the effects of so sudden a breach, and therefore made after him, both to observe his designs and to prevent them. But losing sight of him I was a long time in pursuit to no purpose.»

When I had searched the whole town, I returned to my garret where, the ceremony of kisses being over, I got my boy to a closer embrace and, enjoying my wishes, thought myself happy even to envy. Nor had I done when Ascyltos stole to the door and forcing the bolt found us diverting ourselves. Upon which, clapping his hands, he fell a laughing, and turning me about, "What," said he, "most reverend Gentleman! What were you doing, my brother in iniquity?" Nor was he content with words only, but untying the thong that bound his wallet, he belaboured me heartily, and min-

gling reproaches with his blows: "As you like this, desire a second parting."

«The unexpectedness of the thing made me take no notice of it, but politicly turn it off with a laugh. Otherwise I must have been at loggerheads with my rival, whereas sweetening him with a counterfeit mirth I brought him also to laugh for company. "And you, Encolpius," began he, "are so wrapped in pleasures, you little consider how short our money grows, and what we have left will turn to no account. There's nothing to be got in town this summer-time; we shall have better luck in the country. Let's visit our friends."

«Necessity made me approve his advice as well as conceal the smart of the lash, so, loading Gito with our baggage, we left the city and went to the house of one Lycurgus, a Roman knight, who, because Ascyltos had formerly been his pathic, entertained us handsomely, and the company we met there made our diversions the pleasanter. For first there was Tryphaena, a very beautiful woman, that had come with one Lycas, the owner of a ship and of a small seat that lay next the sea. The delight we received in this place was more than can be expressed, though Lycurgus's table was thrifty enough. You must know we were all promiscuously employed in affairs of love. The fair Tryphaena pleased me and readily inclined to my wishes, but I had scarce given her the courtesy of the house when Lycas, storming to have his old amour slocked from him, accused me at first of underhand dealing, but soon from a rival addressing himself as a lover he pleasantly told me I must repair his damages and plied me hotly. But Tryphaena having my heart I could not lend him an ear. The refusal set him the sharper; he followed me wherever I went and, getting into my chamber at night, when entreaty did no good he fell to downright violence. But I raised such an outcry that I waked the whole house and by the help of Lycurgus got rid of him for that bout.

«At length, perceiving Lycurgus's house was not for his purpose he would have persuaded me to his own, but I rejecting the proffer, he made use of Tryphaena's authority; and she the rather persuaded me to yield to him because she was in hopes of living more at liberty there. I followed, therefore, whither my love led me, but Lycurgus, having renewed his old concern with Ascyltos, would not suffer him to depart. At last we agreed he should stay with Lycurgus and we go with Lycas. Over and beside which, it was concluded that every one of us, as opportunity offered, should pilfer what he could for the common stock.

«Lycas was overjoyed at my consent and so hastened our departure that, taking leave of our friends, we arrived at his house the same day. But in our passage he so ordered the matter that he sat next me and Tryphaena next to Gito, which he purposely contrived to show the notorious lightness of that woman. Nor was he mistaken in her for she presently grew hot upon the boy. I was quickly jealous and Lycas so exactly remarked it to me that he soon confirmed my suspicion of her. On this

I began to be easier to him, which made him all joy, as being assured the unworthiness of my new mistress would beget my contempt of her and, resenting her slight, I should receive him with the better will.

«So stood the matter while we were at Lycas's: Tryphaena was desperately in love with Gito; Gito again as wholly devoted to her; I cared little for the sight of either of them; and Lycas, studying to please me, found me every day some new diversion. In all which also his wife Doris, a fine woman, strove to exceed him and that so gaily that she presently thrust Tryphaena from my heart. I gave her the wink and she returned her consent by as wanton a twinkle so that this dumb rhetoric going before the tongue, secretly conveyed each other's mind.

«I knew Lycas was jealous which kept me tongue-tied so long, and the love he bore his wife made him discover to her his inclination to me. But the first opportunity we had of talking together she related to me what she had learned from him, and I frankly confessed it but withal told her how absolutely averse I had ever been to it. "Well then," quoth the discreet woman, "we must try our wits, according to his own opinion. The permission was one's and the possession another's." By this time Gito had been worn off his legs and was gathering new strength, when Tryphaena came back to me but, disappointed of her expectations, her love turned to a downright fury and, all on fire with following me to no purpose, got into my intrigue both with Lycas and his wife. She made no account of his gamesomeness with me, as well knowing it would hinder no grist to her mill, but for Doris she never left till she had found out our private amours, and gave a hint of it to Lycas. Whose jealousy having got the upper hand of his love ran all to revenge; but Doris, advertised by Tryphaena's woman to divert the storm, forbore any clandestine meetings.

«As soon as I perceived it, having cursed the treachery of Tryphaena and the ingratitude of Lycas, I began to think of retiring and fortune favoured me. For a ship consecrated to the Goddess Isis, laden with rich spoils, had the day before run upon the rocks. Gito and I laid our heads together and he was as willing as myself to be gone, for Tryphaena, having drawn him dry, began now not to be so fond of him. Early next morning, therefore, we marched to sea-ward where with the less difficulty we got on board the ship because we were no strangers to Lycas's servants who at that time took care of her. They still honouring us with their company, it was not a time to filch anything but, leaving Gito with them, I took an opportunity of getting into the stern where the image of Isis stood, and stripped her of a rich mantle and silver trimmings and, also lifting other good booty out of the master's cabin, I stole down a rope, un-seen of any but Gito who also gave them the slip and sneaked after me.

«As soon as I saw him I shewed him the purchase and both of us resolved to make what haste we could to Ascyltos, but Lycurgus's house was not to be reached the same day. When we came to Ascyltos we shewed him the prize and told him in short the manner of getting it and how we had been made the mere make-game of love. He advised us to prepossess Lycurgus with our case and make him our friend ere the others could see him and withal boldly assert it that the ill-usage of Lycas was the only cause why we stole away so hastily. Which when Lycurgus came to understand he swore he would at all times protect us from our enemies.

«Our flight was unknown till Tryphaena and Doris were got out of bed, for we daily attended their levee and waited on them while they were dressing. But when, contrary to our usual custom, they found us missing, Lycas sent after us and especially to the sea-side, for he had heard we made that way, but not a word of the pillage, for the ship lay somewhat to sea-ward and the master had not yet returned on board. But at last, it being taken for granted we had run away, and Lycas, becoming uneasy for want of us, fell desperately foul on his wife whom he supposed to be the cause of our departure. I pass over what words and blows he gave her—I know not every particular—I'll only say Tryphaena, the mother of mischief, had put Lycas in the head that it might so be we had taken sanctuary at Lycurgus's where she persuaded him to go in quest of the fugitives and promised to bear him company that she might confound our impudence with just reproaches.

«The next day they accordingly set forward and came to his house. But we were out of the way, for Lycurgus was gone to a festival in honour of Hercules held at a neighbouring village and had taken us with him. Of which when the others were informed they made what haste they could after us and met us in the portico of the temple. The sight of them very much disordered us. Lycas eagerly complained of our flight to Lycurgus but was received with such a contracted brow and so haughty a look that I grew valiant upon it and, opening my throat, charged him with his beastly attempts upon me, as well at Lycurgus's as in his own house. And Tryphaena, endeavouring to stop my mouth, had her share with him, for I set out her harlotry to the mob who were got about us to hear the scolding. And as a proof of what I said I showed them poor sapless Gito, and myself also, whom that itch of the whore had even brought to our graves.

«The shout of the mob put our enemies so out of

countenance that they went off heavily, but, contriving a revenge and therefore observing how we had put upon Lycurgus, they went back to expect him at his house and set him right again. The solemnity ending later than was expected, we could not reach Lycurgus's that night and therefore he brought us to a half-way house but left us asleep next morning and went home to despatch some business, where he found Lycas and Tryphaena waiting for him, who so ordered the matter with him that they brought him to deliver us up. Lycurgus, naturally barbarous and faithless, began to contrive which way to betray us and sent Lycas to get some help whilst he secured us in the village.

«Thither he came and at his first entry treated us as Lycas had done. After which, wringing his hands together, he upbraided us with the lie we had made of Lycas and, taking Ascyltos from us, locked us up in the room where we were, without so much as hearing him speak in our defence but, carrying him to his house, set a guard upon us till he himself should return. On the road Ascyltos did what he could to mollify Lycurgus but, neither entreaties nor love nor tears doing any good on him, it came into our comrade's head to set us at liberty and, being all on fire at Lycurgus's restiness, refused to bed with him that night, and by that means the more easily put into execution what he had been thinking on.

«The family was in their dead sleep when Ascyltos took our fardels on his shoulders and, getting through a breach in the wall which he had formerly taken notice of, came to the village by break of day. And, meeting no one to stop him he boldly entered it and came up to our chamber, which the guard that was upon us had taken care to secure. But the bar being of wood he easily wrenched it with an iron crow and wakened us, for we soundly snored in spite of all our ill fortune. Our guard had so overwatched themselves that they were fallen into a dead sleep, which was the reason we only waked at the breaking of the door. To be short, Ascyltos came in and briefly told us what he had done for our sakes. On this we got up and as we were rigging ourselves it came into my head to kill the guard and rifle the village. I told Ascyltos my mind. He liked the rifling well enough but disapproved the other proposal and gave us our desired liberty without blood. For, being acquainted with every corner of the house, he picked the lock of an inner room where the moveables lay and, bringing us into it, we lifted what was of most value and got off while it was yet early in the morning, avoiding the common road and not resting till we thought ourselves out of danger.

«Then Ascyltos having got heart again, began to amplify the delight he took in having pillaged Lycurgus, of whose miserableness he complained with just reason. For he had neither paid him for his night's service nor kept a table that had either meat or drink on it, being such a sordid pinch-penny that, notwithstanding his infinite wealth, he denied himself the common necessaries of life.

«Ascyltos would have been for Naples the same day had I not told him how imprudent it was to take up there where, according to all probability, we were most likely to be sought after. "And therefore," said I, "let's keep out of the way for the present, and, since we have enough to keep us from want, stroll it about till the heat be over." The advice was approved and we set forward for a pleasant country town where we were sure to meet some of our acquaintance that were taking the benefit of the season. But we were scarce got half way when a shower of rain, emptying itself upon us like buckets, forced us into the next village where, entering the inn, we saw a great many others that had also been struck in to avoid the storm. The throng kept us from being taken notice of and gave us the opportunity of prying here and there what we might filch in a crowd, when Ascyltos, unheeded of anyone, took a purse from the ground in which he found several pieces of gold. We leaped for joy at so fortunate a beginning but, fearing lest some or other might seek after it, we slunk out at a back door where we saw a groom saddling his horses. But, as having forgotten somewhat, he ran into the house, leaving behind him an embroidered mantle fastened to one of the saddles. In his absence I cut the straps and under the cover of some out-houses we made off with it to a neighbouring forest.

«Being more out of danger among the thickets, we cast about where we should hide the gold, that we might not be either charged with the felony or robbed of it ourselves. At last we concluded to sew it in the lining of an old patched coat which I threw over my shoulders and entrusted the care of the mantle to Ascyltos, with an intent to get to the city by cross-ways. But as we

were going out we heard somebody on our left hand speak to this purpose: "They shall not escape us. They came into the wood. Let's separate ourselves and beat about, that we may the better discover and take them." This put us into such a fright that Ascyltos and Gito fled through briars and brambles towards the city, but I turned back again in such a hurry that, without perceiving it, the precious coat dropped from my shoulders. At last, being quite tired and not able to go any further, I laid me down under the shelter of a tree where I first missed the coat. Then grief restored my strength and up I got again to try if I could recover the treasure. I wandered backwards and forwards to no manner of purpose till, spent and wasted with toil and sorrow, I got into a thicket where, having tarried four hours, and half dead with the horror of the place, I sought the way out but, going forward, a countryman came in sight of me. Then I had need of all my confidence, nor did it fail me. I went up roundly to him and, making my moan how I had lost myself in the wood, desired him to tell me the way to the city. He, pitying my figure, for I was as pale as death and all bemired, asked me if I had seen anyone in the wood. I answered, "Not a soul," on which he courteously brought me into the highway, where he met two of his friends who told him they had traversed the wood through and through but had lit on nothing but a coat which they showed him.

«It may easily be believed I had not the courage to challenge it though I knew well enough what the value of it was. This afflicted me more than all the rest. However, bewailing my treasure, the countryman not heeding me and feebleness growing upon me, I slackened my pace and jogged on slower than ordinarily.

«It was longer ere I reached the city than I thought of, but coming to the inn I found Ascyltos half dead stretched on a straw pallet and fell on another myself, not able to utter a word. He, missing the coat, was in a great disorder and hastily demanded of me what was become of it. I, on the other hand, scarce able to draw my breath, resolved him by my languishing eyes what my tongue would not give me leave to speak. At length, recovering by little and little, I plainly told him the ill-luck I had met with. But he thought I jested and, though the tears in my eyes might have been as full evidence to him as an oath, he yet questioned the truth of what I said and would not believe but I had a mind to cheat him. During this Gito stood as troubled as myself and the boy's sadness increased mine. But the fresh pursuit that was made after us distracted me most. I opened the whole matter to Ascyltos who seemed little concerned at it, as having luckily got off for the present, and withal assured himself that we were past danger in that we were neither known nor seen by anyone. However, it was thought fit to pretend a sickness that we might have the better pretext to keep where we were, but our moneys falling shorter than we thought of, and necessity enforcing us, we found it high time to sell some of our pillage.»

It was almost dark when, going into the brokers' market, we saw abundance of things to be bought and sold; of no extraordinary value, 'tis true, yet such whose night-walking trade the dusk of the evening might easily conceal. We also had the mantle with us and, taking the opportunity of a blind corner, fell a shaking the skirt of it to see if so glittering a show would bring us a purchaser. Nor had we been long there ere a certain coun-

tryman, whom I thought I had seen before, came up to
us with a woman after him and began to consider the
mantle more narrowly, as on the other side did Ascyltos
our country chapman's shoulders, which presently
startled him and struck him dumb. Nor could I myself
behold 'em without being concerned at it, for he seemed
to me to be the same fellow that had found the coat in
the wood; as in truth he was. But Ascyltos, doubting
whether he might trust his eyes or not, and that he
might not do any thing rashly, first came nearer to him
as a buyer and, taking the coat from his shoulders, began
to cheapen and turn it more carefully.

O the wonderful vagaries of Fortune! for the country-
man had not so much as examined a seam of it, but care-
lessly exposed it as beggars' booty. Ascyltos, seeing the
coat unripped and the person of the seller contemptible,
took me aside from the crowd and "Don't you see,
brother," said he, "the treasure I made such a moan
about is returned? That's the coat with the gold in it,
all safe and untouched. What, therefore, shall we do, or
what course shall we take to get our own again?"

I was now comforted, not so much that I had seen the
booty but had cleared myself of the suspicion that lay
upon me, and was by no means for going about the
bush, but downright bringing an action against him,
that if the fellow would not give up the coat to the right-
ful owner, we might recover it by law.

Ascyltos on the other side, afraid of the law; "Who,"
said he, "knows us in this place, or will give any credit to

what we say? I am clear for buying it, though we know it to be our own, and rather recover the treasure with a little money than embroil ourselves in an uncertain suit.

> Laws bear the name; but money has the power.
> The cause is bad whene'er the client's poor.
> Those strict-lived men that seem above our world
> Are oft too modest to resist our gold:
> So judgement, like our other wares, is sold.
> And the grave knight that nods upon the laws,
> Waked by a fee, hems, and approves the cause."

But we had not above a couple of groats ready money, and that we designed should buy us somewhat to eat. Lest, therefore, the coat should be gone in the mean time, we agreed, rather than fail, to sell the mantle at a lower price, that the advantage we got by the one might make what we lost by the other more easy.

As soon, therefore, as we had spread open the mantle, the woman that stood muffled by the countryman, having pryingly taken notice of some tokens about it, forcibly laid both hands on't and, setting up her throat, cried out, "Thieves! Thieves!"

We, on the other part, were very much surprised at the accident, yet, lest we should be wanting to ourselves in this extremity, we got hold of the tattered coat and as spitefully roared out, "They have robbed us of it!" But our case was in no wise like theirs, and the rabble that came in upon the outcry ridiculed, as they are wont, the weaker side, in that the others laid claim to so rich a mantle and we to a ragged coat, scarce worth a good patch. At this Ascyltos could hardly keep his countenance, but the noise being over: "We see," said he, "how everyone likes his own best. Give us our coat and let them take the mantle."

The countryman and the woman liked the exchange well enough, but a sort of pettifoggers, most of whose business was such night practice, having a mind to get the mantle in their own custody, as importunely required that both mantle and coat should be left in their hands, and a judge would determine the cause on the morrow. For it was not the things alone that seemed to be in dispute, but quite another matter to be enquired into—to wit, a strong suspicion of robbery on both sides.

At least it was agreed to put both into some indifferent

hand till the right was determined, when presently one, I know not who, with a bald pate and a face full of pimples, a pettifogging kind of solicitor, steps out of the rout and, laying hold of the mantle, said he'd be security it should be forthcoming the next day—when in truth his intention was that having got it into hucksters' hands it might be smuggled amongst them, as believing we would never come to own it for fear of being taken up for stealing it. For our part we were as willing as he, and an accident befriended both of us. For the countryman, thinking scorn of it that we demanded to have the patched coat given us, threw it at Ascyltos's head and, discharging us of everything but the mantle, required that to be secured as the only cause of the dispute. Having therefore recovered, as we thought, our treasure, we made all the haste we could to the inn and, having shut the door upon us, made ourselves merry as well with the judgement of the rabble as of our detractors, who with so much circumspection had restored us our money.

> What's soon obtained, we nauseously receive;
> All hate the victory that's got with leave.

«While we were ripping the coat and taking out the gold, we overheard somebody asking mine host what kind of people those were that had just now come in. And, being startled at the question, I went down to see what was the matter, and understood that a city sergeant who, according to the duty of his office, took account of all strangers, had seen a couple come into the inn whose names he had not yet registered and therefore enquired of what country they were and what was their way of living. But mine host gave me such a blind account of it that I began to suspect we were not safe there, whereupon, for fear of being taken up, we thought fit to make off for the present and not to return back again till it was late in the night, but leave the care of our supper to Gito. We had resolved to keep out of the broad streets and accordingly took our walk through that quarter of the city where we were likely to meet least company when, in a narrow winding lane which had no passage through, we saw somewhat before us two handsome well dressed ladies. We followed them at a distance to a chapel which they entered and from whence we heard an odd humming kind of noise as it came from the hollow of a cave. Curiosity also made us go in after them, where we saw a number of women, as mad as if they had been sacrificing to Bacchus, each of them with the ensign of Priapus in her hand. More than that we could not get to see, for they no sooner perceived us than they set up such a shout that the roof of the temple shook again, and withal endeavoured to lay hands on us. But we scampered away and made what haste we could to the inn.»

We had scarce eaten the supper which Gito had got ready for us when a more than ordinary knocking at the door put us into another fright, and when we, pale as death, asked who was there, answer was made: "Open the door and you'll see." While we were yet talking, the bolt dropped off and fell down of its own accord and the door miraculously flew open, on which a woman with her head veiled came in upon us, the very same who a little before was with the countryman in the market, and "What," said she, "do you think to put a trick upon me? I am Quartilla's maid, whose sacred recess you so lately disturbed. She is at the inn-gate and desires to speak with you. You need not be uneasy; she neither blames your inadvertency or has a mind to resent it, but rather wonders what God brought such civil gentlemen into her quarters."

We were silent as yet and gave her the hearing, but not the least inclined to grant any part of her requests, when in came Quartilla herself, attended with a young girl and, sitting down by me, fell a weeping. Nor here also did we offer a word, but stood expecting what would be the event of these tears which she commanded at her discretion. At last, when the shower had emptied itself, she disdainfully turned up her hood, and wringing her hands together till the joints were ready to crack, "What impudence," said she, "is this? Or where learnt you these shams and that sleight of hand you have so lately been beholden to? By my faith, I am sorry for ye, for no one beheld what was unlawful for him to see and went off unpunished. And verily our part of the town hath so many deities, you'll sooner find a God than a man in it. Don't believe I come here with any sentiments of revenge; I am more concerned for your youth than angry at the injuries you have done me; for unawares as yet, I think, you have committed an unexpiable abomination.

"For my part it troubled me all night and threw me into such a shaking that I was afraid I had gotten a tertian ague, on which I took somewhat to have made me sleep, but the God appeared to me and commanded me to rise and find you out as the likeliest way to take off the violence of the fit. But I am not so much in pain for a remedy as that a greater anguish strikes me to the heart and will undoubtedly make an end of me, for fear in one of your youthful frolics you should declare what you saw in Priapus's chapel and disclose the Mysteries of the Gods among the vulgar. Low as your knees I therefore lift my hands t'ye, that you neither make sport of our night worship nor dishonour the rites of so many years which 'tis not everyone, even among ourselves, that knows."

After this she fell a crying again, and with many a pitiful groan fell flat on my bed, when I at the same time, between pity and fear, bid her take courage and assure herself of both; for that we would neither divulge these holy Mysteries, nor, if the God had prescribed her any other remedy for her ague, be wanting ourselves to assist Providence, even with our own hazard.

At this promise of mine, becoming more cheerful, she fell a kissing me thick and threefold, and changing her tears into laughing she combed up some hair that hung over my face with her fingers and, "I come to a truce with you," said she, "and discharge you of the process I intended against you. But if you should refuse me the medicine I entreat of you for the ague, I have fellows enough will be ready by to-morrow who shall both vindicate my reputation and revenge the affront you put upon me.

> Contempt's uncivil, to command is rude;
> Love does no force upon the fair intrude.
> The best revenge is to neglect an ill;
> The wise forgive—or kissing, kindly kill."

Then, clapping her hands together, she fell into so violent a fit of laughter that she made us apprehensive of some design against us; the same also did the woman that came in first and the girl that came with her.

Their mirth seemed so odd and unnatural that we, who saw no reason for so sudden a change, stood amazed and sometimes looked upon the women and sometimes upon one another.

At length quoth Quartilla, "I have commanded that no flesh alive be suffered to come into this inn to-day, that I may receive from you the medicine for my ague without interruption." At this Ascyltos was a little amazed and I so chilled that I had not the power to utter a word; but the company gave me heart not to expect worse, for they were but three women and, if they had any design, must yet be too weak to effect it against us who, if we had nothing more of man about us, had yet that figure to befriend us. We were all girt up for the purpose, and I had so contrived the order of battle that if it must come to a rencounter I was to make my part

good with Quartilla, Ascyltos with her woman, and Gito with the girl.

«While I was thus contriving the matter, Quartilla came up to me to cure her of her ague but, finding herself disappointed, flew off in a rage and, returning in a little while, commanded some persons in disguise to remove us into a noble palace.»

Here all our courage failed us and nothing but certain death seemed to appear before us. . . .

When I began, "If, Madam, you design to be more severe with us, be yet so kind as to dispatch us quickly, for the nature of our offence is not so heinous that we ought to be racked to death for it. . . .

Upon which her woman, whose name was Psyche, spread a carpet on the floor. . . .

She fell examining the inside of my breeches, but her labour was lost, all was quite gone. . . .

Ascyltos muffled his head in his coat, as having had a hint given him how dangerous it was to take notice of what did not concern him. . . .

In the meantime Psyche took off her garters, and with one of them bound our feet and with the other our hands. . . .

«Thus fettered as I lay, "Madam," said I, "this is not the way to make me capable of ridding you of your ague." "I grant it," answered Psyche, "but I have a dose at hand will infallibly do it," and thereupon she brought me a lusty bowl of satyricon (a love potion) and so merrily ran over the wonderful effects of it, that I had well-nigh sucked it all off. But because Ascyltos had slighted her addresses, she, finding his back towards her, threw what was left on him.»

Ascyltos perceiving the chat was at an end, "Am I not worthy," said he, "to get a sup?" And Psyche, discovered by my laughter, clapped her hands and told him, "Young man, I made you an offer of it, but your friend here has just now drunk it all up." "Is it so?" said Quartilla, "and has Encolpius gulped it all down?" . . . . and shook her sides with very agreeable laughter. . . .

At last even Gito laughed for company, at what time the young wench flung her arms about his neck and, meeting no resistance, half smothered him with kisses. . . .

We would have cried out, but there was no one near

to help us, and as I was offering to bid 'em keep the peace, Psyche fell a pricking my cheeks with her bodkin. On the other side also, the young wench half stifled Ascyltos with a dish-clout she had rubbed in the bowl. . . .

Lastly came leaping upon us a bugger in a belted velvet mantle stuck with myrtle, and one while almost ground our buttocks to powder, and other while slobbered us with his nasty kisses, till Quartilla, holding a whalebone whip in her hand and her petticoats girt high, discharged us of the service. . . .

We both took a most solemn oath that so dreadful a secret should go no further than ourselves. . . .

Then came in a company of tumblers and rubbed us over with the yolk of an egg beaten to oil, when, being somewhat refreshed, we put on our dinner clothes and were led into the next room that had three rich beds in it and the rest of the entertainment as splendidly set out. The word was given and we sat down, when, having whet our appetites with an excellent antipast, we swilled ourselves with the choicest wine, nor was it long ere we fell a nodding. "Is it so," quoth Quartilla, "can ye sleep when ye know it is the vigil to Priapus?". . . .

At what time Ascyltos snored so soundly that Psyche, not yet forgetting the disappointment he gave her, all besooted his face and scored down his lips and shoulders with a burnt stick's end.

Plagued with these mischiefs, I hardly got the least wink of sleep; nor was the whole family, whether with-

in doors or without, in a much better condition. Some
lay up and down at our feet, others had run their heads
against the walls, and others lay dead asleep across the
threshold; the lamps also, having drunk up all their oil,
gave a weak and glimmering light.

At this instant got in a couple of Syrian rogues to have
stolen our wine, but while they fell a scuffling among
some silver vessels that stood upon the table they broke
the earthen jar that held the wine and overthrew a table
with some plate on it. At the same time also a cup, fall-
ing off the shelf on Psyche's bed, broke her head as she
lay fast asleep, upon which she cried out and therewith
discovered the thieves and waked some of the drunkards.
The thieves, on the other hand, finding themselves in
danger of discovery, threw themselves on one of the
beds, as though they were guests, and fell a snoring as
soundly as the rest. The usher of the hall, being by this
time got awake, put some more oil into the dying
lamps, and the boys, having rubbed their eyes, returned
to their charge; when in came a woman dancer with
cymbals, and the clashing of the brass roused all the rest.

On which the banquet was renewed, and Quartilla
gave the word to go on where we left off drinking; the
cymbal-dancer also added not a little to our midnight
revel. . . .

At last bolted in a most shameless bugger, void of
grace both in words and action and truly worthy of the
house where he was, who, having composed himself in
an affected manner, mouthed out these verses:

O yes! Now buggers with your wanton tricks
Make haste, move your legs quick, make the ground drum;
With wanton arms, soft thighs, and active hips,
The old, the tender, and the sweetly young!

Having done with his poetry, he smeared my lips with
his filthy kisses, then getting on the bed, overcame my
resistance and bared my breech. Long and hard he toiled
at my groin, but 'twas all in vain. Great drops of paint
hung like gum on his forehead and came trickling down
the wrinkles of his cheeks like rain on a new plastered
wall.

Nor could I forbear tears any longer, but being
brought to the last extremity, "I beseech you, Madam,"
says I, "did you not tell us we should see the fairies?"
Gently clapping her hands, "A very witty gentleman,"
said she, "a man of excellent parts! What? Don't you
know these sort of people are called fairies?" Upon this,
that my companion might not 'scape better than myself,
"By your integrity, Madam," said I, "does Ascyltos alone
keep holyday among us?" "Even so," said she, "let him
have his share too!" And therewith the rascal changed
his mount and turning to Ascyltos with tricks and kisses
almost beat him to powder.

Gito stood laughing all the while till he had well-nigh
split himself, which Quartilla perceiving, with much
curiosity enquired whose boy he was. And, I telling her
he was my comrade, "Why then," said she, "has he not
kissed me?" And so calling him to her, she fell to kissing
him smartly, then toying with his little tool. "This,"

said she, "may do well enough for a whet, and get me an appetite to-morrow; but having made so full a meal already, it is not my way to put a churl on a gentleman."

With that, Psyche came tittering to her and, having whispered I know not what in her ear, "You are in the right on't," quoth Quartilla, " 'twas well thought on! Since we have so fine an opportunity, why should not our Pannychis lose her maidenhead?" And forthwith was brought in a pretty young girl that seemed not to be above seven years of age and was the same that came into our inn with Quartilla. All approving the design and desiring the consummation, a match was struck up between the boy and her. For my part I stood amazed, and assured them that neither Gito, a most bashful lad, was able for the drudgery, nor the girl of years to receive it. "Is that all?" quoth Quartilla. "Is she less than I was when I first entered on't? I vow by all that's good, I can't remember I was ever a maid. For when I was in hanging-sleeves I went to creep-mouse with the little boys, and as I grew in years I entertained myself with bigger, till I came to the age you see. And truly I think hence came the proverb: she'll bear him a bull that bore him a calf." Fearing therefore my comrade might run a greater hazard by my delay, I got up to the wedding.

———And now Psyche put a flame-coloured veil upon the girl's head, the pathic led before with the flambeau, and a long train of drunken women fell a shouting and dressed up the bride-chamber. Quartilla, all agog as the rest of us, took hold of Gito and dragged him into the room. But truly the boy made no resistance, nor seemed the girl frightened at the name of matrimony. When, therefore, they were locked up we sat without before the threshold of the chamber, and Quartilla, having waggishly slit a chink in the door, as wantonly laid an ape's eye to it. Nor content with that, plucked me also to see that child's play and, when we were not peeping, would turn her lips to me and steal a kiss.

«The jade's fulsomeness had so tired me that I began to devise which way to get off. I told Ascyltos my mind and he was well pleased with it for he was as willing to get rid of his torment, Psyche. This might easily have been done if Gito had not been locked up in the chamber. For we were resolved to take him with us and not leave him to the mercy of a bawdy house. While we were contriving how to effect it, it so happened that Pannychis fell out of bed and drew Gito with her without being hurt. But the girl got a small knock as she fell and therewith made such a cry that Quartilla, all in a fright, ran headlong in and gave us the opportunity of getting off and taking the boy with us. When without more ado we flew to our inn» and getting to bed passed the rest of the night without fear.

«But going out the next day whom should we meet but two of those fellows that robbed us of the mantle. Which Ascyltos perceiving, he briskly attacked one of them and, having disarmed and desperately wounded him, came in to my assistance who was pressing hard upon the other. But he behaved himself so well that he wounded us both, although but slightly, and got off himself without so much as a scratch.»

And now came the third day, that is the expectation of a dinner by ourselves, but having received some wounds, we thought flight might be of more use to us than sitting still. «We got to our inn, therefore, as fast as we could, and our wounds not being great, cured them as we lay in bed, with wine and oil.

«But the rogue whom Ascyltos had hewn down lay in the street, and we were in fear of being discovered;» while therefore we were pensively considering which way to avoid the impending storm, a servant of Agamemnon's interrupted our fears. "And don't you know," said he, "with whom you are to eat to-day? Trimalchio, a trim finical humorist, has a clock in his dining room and an army trumpeter to let him know how many minutes of his life he has lost." We therefore dressed ourselves carefully, and Gito willingly taking upon him the part of a servant, as he had hitherto done, we bade him put our things together and follow us to the bath.

We rambled up and down, fully dressed, we knew not where; or rather, having a mind to divert us, struck into a tennis-court, where we saw an old bald-pated fellow in a carnation-coloured coat playing at ball with a company of boys. Nor was it so much the boys, though it was worth our while to observe them, that engaged our attention, as the master of the house himself in pumps, who altogether tossed the ball and never struck it after it once came to the ground, but had a servant by him with a bag full of them, and enough for all that played.

We observed also other new things, for in the gallery stood two eunuchs, one of whom held a silver chamber-pot, the other counted the balls; not those they kept tossing, but such as fell to the ground. While we admired the humour, one Menelaus came up to us and told us, "This is the gentleman you must sup with to-night," and that we had seen the beginning of our entertainment. As he was yet talking, Trimalchio snapped his fingers, at which sign the eunuch held the chamber-pot to him as he was playing. Having eased himself and called for water, he dipped the tips of his fingers in it and dried them on the boy's head. 'Twould be too long to lay open the whole scene: we went into the Hummums and, being presently in a sweat, we descended into a cold

bath. And while Trimalchio was anointed from head to foot with a liquid perfume and rubbed clean again, not with linen, but the finest flannel, his three rubbers plied stoutly some bottles of rich muscadine. When they fell to brawling over their cups, Trimalchio said they were drinking his health. Then wrapped in a mantle of scarlet velvet he was laid on a litter borne by six servants, with four lackeys in rich liveries running before him, and by his side a sedan in which was carried his darling, a blear-eyed overgrown boy, more ill-favoured than his master, Trimalchio. As he went along, a flute player kept close to his ear with a flageolet, as if he had whispered him, and made him music all the way.

Wondering, we followed, and, with Agamemnon, came to the gate on which hung a tablet with this inscription:

WHATEVER SERVANT GOES OUT
WITHOUT HIS MASTER'S LEAVE
SHALL RECEIVE A HUNDRED STRIPES.

In the porch stood the porter in a green livery girt about with a cherry-coloured girdle, cleansing of peas in a silver charger; and overhead hung a golden cage with a magpie in it which gave us an All Hail as we entered. But while I was gaping at these novelties I had like to have broken my neck backwards, for on the left hand, not far from the porter's lodge, there was a great dog in a chain painted on the wall, and over him, written in capital letters, BEWARE THE DOG. My companions could not forbear laughing, but I, recollecting my spirits, pursued my design of going to the end of the wall. It contained the draught of a market-place where slaves were bought and sold, with bills tacked upon them shewing their price. There was also Trimalchio with a white staff in his hand, and Minerva with a train after her entering Rome. A little farther was represented after what manner he had learnt to cast accounts and how he was made auditor, all exquisitely painted with their proper explanations; and, at the end of the gallery, Mercury lifting him by the chin and placing him on a judgement seat. Fortune stood by him with a cornucopia, and the three fatal sisters spinning a golden thread.

I observed also in the same place a troop of running footmen, with their commander exercising them, as also a large armory, in one of the angles of which stood a shrine with the Gods of the House in silver, a marble statue of Venus, and a large golden box in which it was said he kept the first shavings of his beard. We enquired of the servant that had charge of these things what pictures were those in the middle. "The Iliads and the Odyssies," said he, "and the gladiator show of Laenas."

We could not bestow much time to consider them, for by this time we were come to the dining-room, in the entry of which sat the steward inspecting accounts. But what I most admired were those bundles of rods with their axes, that were fastened to the sides of the door, and stood, as it were, on the brazen prow of a ship, on which was written:

TO CAIUS POMPEIUS TRIMALCHIO
A MAN OF QUALITY
CINNAMUS THE STEWARD.

Under the same title also hung a lamp with two branches from the roof of the room, and two tablets on either side of the door, of which one, if I well remember, had this inscription:

THE THIRD AND SECOND DAY
BEFORE THE KALENDS OF JANUARY
OUR LORD CAIUS EATS ABROAD.

On the other was represented the course of the moon and the seven planets, and what days were lucky or unlucky, with an embossed stud to distinguish the one from the other.

Full of this luxury we were now entering the room where one of his boys, set there for that purpose, called aloud to us: "Right feet first!" Nor is it to be doubted, but we were somewhat concerned for fear of breaking the orders of the place. But while we were footing it accordingly, a servant stripped of his livery fell at our feet and besought us to save him from a whipping, for he said his fault was no great matter, but that some clothes of the steward's had been stolen from him in the bath, and all of them not worth eighteen pence. We returned, therefore, in good decorum and finding the steward in the counting house telling some gold, besought him to remit the servant's punishment. When putting on a haughty face, "It is not," said he, "the loss of the thing that troubles me, but the negligence of this careless rascal. He has lost me the garments I used to feast in and which a client of mine presented me with on my birthday. Right true Tyrian purple, of course, but already once cleaned. Yet whatever it be, I grant your request."

Having received so great a favour, as we were entering the dining-room, the servant for whom we had been suitors met us and, kissing us, who stood wondering what the humour meant, over and over gave us thanks for our civility, and in short told us we should know by and by whom it was we had obliged: "The wine which my Lord keeps for his own drinking is in the disposition of his butler."

At length we sat down, when some gypsy boys coming about us, some of them poured snow water on our hands, and others pared the nails of our feet with a mighty dexterity, and that not silently but singing as it were by the bye. I resolved to try if the whole family sang, and therefore called for drink, which one of the boys as readily brought me, with an odd kind of tune, and the same did everyone as you asked for anything. You'd have taken it for a morris-dancers' Hall, not the table of a person of quality.

Then came a sumptuous antipast, for we were all seated, but only Trimalchio, for whom, after a new fashion, the chief place was reserved. Besides that, there was set by us a large platter of Corinthian bronze with a little donkey with two panniers in one of which were white olives, in the other black. Two broad pieces of plate covered the vessel, on the brims of which were engraven Trimalchio's name and the weight of the silver, with little bridges soldered together and on them dormice strewed over with honey and poppy. There were also piping hot sausages on a silver gridiron, and under that large damsons with the kernels of pomegranates.

In this condition we were when Trimalchio himself was waddled in to the strains of the chorus, and being close bolstered with neckcloths and pillows to keep off the air, we could not forbear laughing in spite of our teeth. For his bald pate peeped out of a scarlet mantle, and over the load of cloths he lay under there hung an embroidered towel with purple tassels and fringes dingle dangle about it. He had also on the little finger of his left hand a large gilt ring, and on the extreme joint of the finger next it, one lesser, which I took for all gold, but at last it appeared to be jointed together with a kind of stars of steel. And that we might see these were not all his bravery he stripped his right arm, on which he wore a golden bracelet and an ivory circle, bound together with a glittering locket and a medal at the end of it. Then, picking his teeth with a silver pin, "I had not, my friends," said he, "any inclination to have come among you so soon, but, fearing my absence might make you wait too long, I denied myself my own satisfaction.

However, suffer me to make an end of my game." There followed him a boy with an inlaid table of terebinth wood and crystal dice, and I took notice of one thing more pleasant than the rest, for instead of black and white counters, his were all silver and gold pieces of money.

In the mean time, while he was squandering his heap at play and we were yet picking a bit here and there, a cupboard was brought in with a basket in which was a hen carved in wood, her wings lying round and hollow as sitting on brood. When presently the concert struck up and two servants fell a searching the straw under her, and, taking out some peahen's eggs, distributed them round the company. At this Trimalchio, changing countenance, "I commanded, my friends," said he, "the hen to be set with peahen's eggs, and, so help me Hercules, I'm afraid they are half hatched; however, we'll try if they are yet fit to be eaten." Whereupon we received spoons of at least six pounds weight with which we easily broke the shell, made of paste and moulded into the figure of an egg. And for my own part, I was like to have thrown away my share, for it seemed to me to have a chick in it; till hearing an old guest of that table say, "It must be some good bit or other," I searched further into it and found a delicate fat wheatear in the middle of a well peppered yolk.

On this, Trimalchio stopped his play for a while, and asking the like for himself declared if any of us would have more metheglin, it was at our service, when of a

sudden the music gave the sign and the first course was scrambled away by a company of singers and dancers. But in the rustle it happening that a dish fell on the floor, a boy took it up, and Trimalchio, taking notice of it, gave him a box on the ear and commanded him to throw it down again; and presently the Groom of the Chamber came with a broom and swept away the silver dish with whatever else had fallen from the table.

When presently came in two long-haired blacks with small leather bottles, such as they carry sand in to strew on the stage, and gave us wine to wash our hands, but no one offered us water. We all admiring the finicalness of the entertainment, "Mars," said he, "is a lover of Justice, and therefore let every one have a table to himself; for having more elbow room, these nasty stinking boys will be less troublesome to us." And thereupon

large double-eared vessels of glass, close plastered over, were brought up, with labels about their necks upon which was this inscription:

OPIMIAN MUSCADINE OF AN
HUNDRED YEARS OLD.

While we were reading the titles Trimalchio clapped his hands and "Alas! Alas!" said he, "that wine should live longer than man! Wherefore let us make merry. Wine is life. 'Tis right Opimian. I brought not out so good yesterday, yet there were persons of better quality supped with me!"

We drank and admired everything, when in came a servant with a silver puppet, a skeleton so jointed and put together that it turned every way; and being more than once thrown upon the table, cast itself into several figures, on which Trimalchio came out with his poetry:

Unhappy mortals! on how fine a thread
Our lives depend! How like this puppet-man
Shall we, alas! be all when we are dead!
Therefore let's live merrily while we can.

The applause we gave him was followed with a service but, respecting the place, not so considerable as might have been expected. However, the novelty of the thing drew every man's eye upon it. It was a large charger with the twelve signs of the Zodiac round it, upon every one of which the master-cook had laid somewhat or other suitable to the sign: upon Aries, a sort of peas which resembled a ram's head; upon Taurus, a piece of beef; upon Gemini, a pair of pendulums and kidneys; upon Cancer, a coronet; upon Leo, an African fig; upon the Virgin, a sow's womb; upon Libra, a pair of scales in one of which was a tart, in the other a custard; upon Scorpio, a pilchard; upon Sagittary, a crow; upon Capricorn, a lobster; upon Aquarius, a goose; upon Pisces, two mullets. And in the middle a plat of herbs, cut like a green turf, and over them a honey-comb. During this, a black boy carried about bread in a silver oven and with a hideous voice forced a bawdy song from the mime called Assafoetida.

When Trimalchio perceived we looked awry on such coarse fare, "Come, come," said he, "fall to; this is our manner of eating." Nor had he sooner uttered these words than the concert struck up and four waiters fell a dancing and took off the upper part of the charger, under which was a dish of crammed fowl, and the hinder paps of a sow that had farrowed but the day before, and in the middle, a hare, stuck round with feathers that he looked like a flying horse. On the sides of the dish there were four little images that spouted a relishing sauce on some fish that lay near them as in a canal.

We also seconded the shout begun by the family and fell merrily aboard this; and Trimalchio, no less pleased than ourselves, cried, "Cut!" At which the music sounding again, the carver humoured it, and cut up the meat with such antic postures you'd have thought him a carman fighting to the music of an organ. Nevertheless, Trimalchio in a lower note, cried out again, "Cut! Cut!" I, hearing the word so often repeated, suspecting there might be some joke in it, was not ashamed to ask him that sat next above me what it meant. And he that had been often present at the like, "You see," said he, "him that carves about; his name is Cutter. And as often as he says, 'Cut!' he both calls and commands."

The humour spoiled my stomach for eating, but turning to him that I might learn more, I talked pleasantly to him at a distance, and at last asked him who that woman was that so often scuttled up and down the room.

"It is," said he, "Trimalchio's wife. Her name is Fortunata. She counts her money by the bushel, but what was she not long since? Pardon me, Sir, you would not have touched her with a pair of tongs. But now, no one knows why or wherefore, she's, as 'twere, got into heaven, and is Trimalchio's all in all. In short, if she says it is midnight at midday he'll believe her. He's so very wealthy he can't tell his riches, but that old cat has an eye everywhere, and when you least think to meet her, she's at your elbow. She's as dry as a bone, careful, full of good counsel, worth her weight in gold, but a very scold, a mere pye at his bolster. Whom she loves, she loves; and whom she does not love, she does not love. Then for Trimalchio, he has more lands than a crow can fly over, moneys upon moneys. There lies more silver in his porter's lodge than any one man's whole estate. And for his family—hey-day! hey-day!—there is not, so help me Hercules, one tenth of them that know their master. In brief, there is not one of these fools about him but he can change him into a cabbage stalk. Nor has he occasion to buy anything; he has all at his own door: wool, lemons, pepper. Nay, do but beat about for hen's milk and you'll find it. In a word, time was his wool was none of the best and therefore he bought rams at Tarentum to mend his breed. As in like manner, to have Attic honey at home, he brought bees from Athens; and besides they improved the natives. It is not long since but he sent to the Indies for mushroom seed. Nor has he so much as a mule that did not come of a wild ass. See you all these quilts? There is not one of them whose wadding is not the finest combed wool, of violet or scarlet colour, dyed in grain. O happy man!

"But have a care how you put a slight on these freedmen, they are rich rogues. Look on him that sits at the lower end of the table; he has now his eight hundred thousand, and 'tis not long since he was not worth a groat and carried billets and faggots on his back. It is said —I know nothing of it myself but by hearsay—he stole the wishing cap of an Incubus and found a treasure. For my part I envy no man—if I get anything it is a bit and a knock. But he still stinks of the kitchen and is well pleased with himself. He lately set up this proclamation:

C. POMPEIUS DIOGENES HAS

SOME LODGINGS TO LET,

FOR HE HATH BOUGHT A HOUSE.

"But what think you of him who sits in the freedman's place? How well was he once! I do not upbraid him; he was worth a million but has not now a hair of his head which is not mortgaged. Nor, so help me Hercules, is it his own fault. There is not a better humoured man than himself, but those rascally freedmen have cheated him of all. For know, when the pot no longer boils, and a man's estate declines, farewell friends! And what trade do you think he drove? He was an undertaker and by that he ate like a prince: wild boars served up whole, all sorts of pastry, wild fowl, and cooks for each sort of provision. More wine was spilt under his table than most men have in their cellars: a mere phantasm. And when his estate was going, and he feared his creditors might fall upon him, he made an auction under this title:

JULIUS PROCULUS WILL MAKE AN AUCTION

OF SEVERAL GOODS HE HAS NO USE OF."

The dish was by this time taken away, and the guests, grown mellow, began to talk of what was done abroad, when Trimalchio broke in on us and interrupted the discourse. Leaning on his elbow, "This wine," said he, "is worth drinking, and fish must swim. But do you think I am satisfied with that part of your supper you saw in the charger? 'Is Ulysses no better known?' What then? We ought to exercise our brains as well as our chaps, and show we are not only lovers of learning but understand it. Peace rest my old master's bones, who made me a man among men. Nobody can tell me anything that is new to me, as that dish has just shown. This heaven, that's inhabited by the Twelve Gods, turns itself into as many figures, and now 'tis Aries. He that is born under that sign has much cattle, much wool, and to that is a blockhead, a brazen-face, and will certainly be a cuckold. There are many scholars, advocates and horned beasts come into the world under this sign." We praised our nativity-caster's pleasantness, and he went on again: "The whole heaven then turns into Taurus, and no wonder it bore football players, herdsmen, and such as can shift for themselves. Under Gemini are often foaled coach horses, oxen calved, great baubles, and such as can claw both sides. I was born myself under Cancer, and therefore stand on many feet, as having large possessions both by sea and land; for Cancer suits one as well as the other and therefore I put nothing upon him that I might not press my own geniture. Under Leo, spendthrifts and bullies; under Virgo, women, runagates and such as wear iron garters; under Libra, butchers, apothecaries and men of business; under Scorpio, poisoners and cut-throats; under Sagittary, such as are goggle-eyed, who while looking at herbs lick suet; under Capricorn, poor helpless rascals, to whom nature bequeathed horns to defend themselves; under Aquarius, cooks and paunch-bellies; under Pisces, caterers and orators. And so the world goes round like a mill, and is never without its mischief, that men be either born or perish. But for that sod of turf in the middle and the honey-comb upon it, I have good reason for that too: Our Mother the Earth is in the middle, made like an egg, and has all good things in herself, like a honey-comb."

"Most learnedly!" we all cried and, lifting our hands, swore neither Hipparchus nor Aratus were to be compared to him, till at last other servants came in and spread coverlets on the beds, on which were painted nets, men in ambush with hunting spears, and whatever appertained to hunting. Nor could we yet tell what to make of it, when we heard a great cry without, and a pack of beagles came in and ran round the table. After this frolic was over, a large tray was set before us, and in it a mighty boar with a cap on his head (such as slaves at their making free, have set on theirs in token of liberty). On his tusks hung two wicker baskets, the one full of fresh dates, the other of dry. And about him lay little pigs of marchpane, as if they were at suck. They signified a sow had farrowed, and hung there as presents for the guests to carry home with them.

To the cutting up this boar there came not he that had served up the fowl before, but a two-handed fellow with a swinging long beard, buskins on his legs, and a short embroidered coat, who, drawing his wood-knife, made a large hole in the boar's side, out of which flew a number of thrushes which were caught in a trice as they fluttered about the room by some fowlers who stood in readiness for the purpose. On which Trimalchio ordered to every man his bird and "See," said he, "what kind of acorns this wild boar fed on!" And presently the boys took off the baskets and distributed the dates among the guests.

In the meantime I, who had private thoughts of my own, was much concerned to know why the boar was brought in with a cap on his head; and therefore, having run out my tittle-tattle, I told my interpreter what troubled me. To which he answered: "Your boy can even tell you what it means, for there's no riddle in it, but it's as clear as day. This boar stood the last of yester-night's supper and dismissed by the guests returns now as a free man among us." I curst myself for a blockhead, and asked him no more questions, that I might not be thought to have never before eaten with men of fashion.

While we were yet talking, in came a handsome boy with a wreath of vine leaves and ivy about his head, calling himself now and then Bromius, another time Lyaeus, and another Euhius, and carried about with him a salver of grapes and with a clear voice repeated some of his master's poetry. At which Trimalchio, turning to

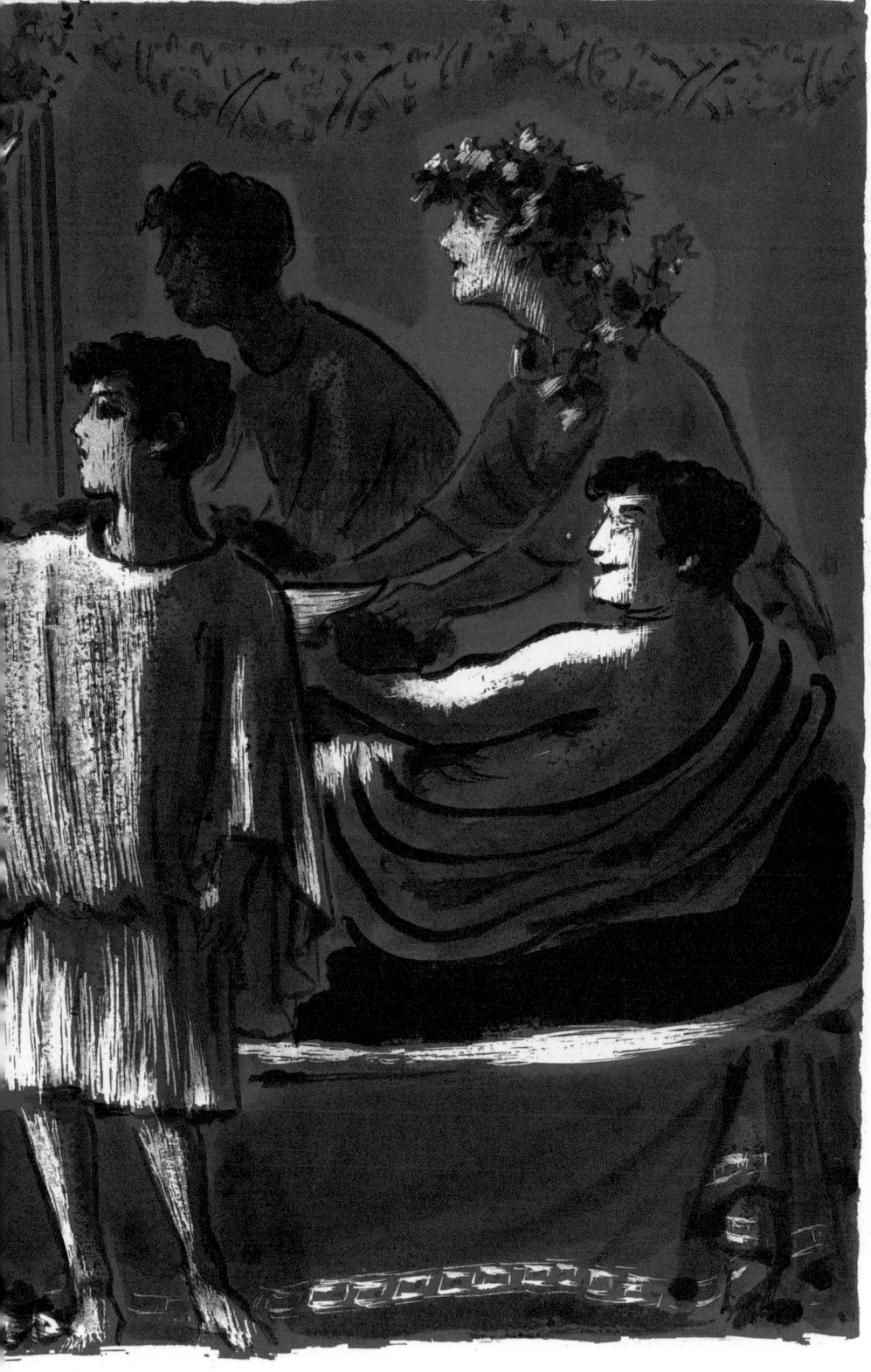

him, "Dionysus," said he, "be thou Father Free!" Whereupon the boy took the cap from off the boar's head and, putting it on his own, Trimalchio added, "You will not deny me, but I have a free father." We all praised the conceit, and soundly kissed the boy as he went round us.

This scene being over, Trimalchio rose up and went to the close-stool. We also being left at liberty without a tyrant fell to some table talk. When presently one calling for a bumper, "The day," said he, "is nothing. 'Tis night before a cat can lick her ear, and therefore nothing is better than to go straight from bed to board. We have had a great deal of frost, the bagnio has scarce heated me; but a warm drink is meat, drink, and clothes. For my part I have spun this day's thread, the wine is got into my noddle, and I am downright Dunstable—"

Then Seleucus took up the cudgels. "And I," said he, "do not bathe every day: the rubber is a mere fuller, cold water has teeth in it and my head grows every day more washy than others, but when I have got my dose in my guts, I bid defiance to the cold. Nor, faith, could I well have bathed to-day: I was at a funeral. That honest fellow, Crysanthus, has breathed his last. Well, rest his soul, 'tis not long since we were together, and methinks I talk with him now. Alas, alas! We are but blown-up bladders! We are less than flies, they yet have somewhat in them, but we are mere bubbles. You'll say he would not be ruled, yet not a drop of water or a crumb of bread went down his throat for five days. And yet he's gone! Some say he died of the Doctor, but I am of opinion his time was come, for a physician is a mere comfort to the mind. However, he was decently carried out of his house with a rich pall over the coffin, and mightily lamented—he made some of his servants free—but his wife seemed little troubled. You'll say again, he was not kind to her; but women are a kind of kites—whatever good is done them, 'tis the same as if it were thrown in a well, and old love is as bad as a gaol."

He grew troublesome and Phileros cried out: "Let us remember the living! He had what was due to him; as he lived well, so he died well, and what has he now that any man moans the want of? He came from nothing, and to his dying day would have taken a farthing from a dunghill with his teeth. Therefore, as he grew up, he grew like a honey-comb. He died worth the Lord knows what, all ready money. But to the matter: I have eaten a dog's tongue and dare speak the truth. He had a foul mouth, was all babble; a very make-bate, not a man. His brother was a brave fellow, a friend to his friends, of an open hand and kept a full table. He did not order his affairs so well at first as he might have done, but the first vintage made him up again, for he sold what wine he would. And what kept up his chin was the expectation of a reversion, the credit of which brought him more than was left him. But his brother taking a pett at him, devised the estate to I know not what bastard. He flies far that flies his relations. Besides, this brother of his had whisperers about him, that were back-friends to the other; but he shall never do right that is quick of belief, especially in matters of business. And yet, 'tis true, he'll be counted wise while he lives to whom the thing, whatever it be, is given, not he that ought to have had it. He was, without doubt, one of Fortune's sons; lead in his hand would turn to gold—and without trouble too, where there are not rubbs in the way. And how many years think you he lived? Seventy odd. But he was as hard as horn, bore his age well, and as black as a crow. I have known him for years, and to his last a good woman's man—verily, I do believe he left not a bitch in his house alone. He was also a great whore-master, all was grist that came to his mill. Nor do I condemn him for it, for this is all he carried with him."

Thus Phileros, and Ganymedes as followeth: "You talk of what concerns neither heaven nor earth, when in the meantime no man regards what makes all victuals so scarce. I could not—so help me Hercules—get a mouthful of bread to-day. And how? The drought continues; for my part I have not filled my belly this twelvemonth. A plague on these clerks of the market; the bakers and they juggle together—claw me and I'll claw thee— which makes the poorer sort starve, while these greater jaw-bones make holiday all year. Oh, that we had those lions I found here, when I first came out of Asia! That had been to live! Were there a scarcity of Sicilian grain, they so handled these clowns they thought Jupiter himself was after them. I remember Safinius; when I was a boy he lived by the Old Arch; you'd have taken him for a pepper-corn rather than a man. Wherever he went the earth parched under him. Yet he was an honest fellow at bottom, one might depend on him, a friend to his friend, and whom you might boldly trust in the dark. But how did he behave himself on the Bench? He carried all things before him, made no starched speeches, but downright. But at the Bar his voice swelled like a trumpet, without sweating or spueing. I fancy he had somewhat, I know not what, of the Asian humour. Then so ready to return a salute and call every one by his name, as if he had been one of us. In his time corn was as cheap as loam, the loaf you bought for a half-penny was more than any two could eat; now I have seen bull's eyes that were larger. Alas! alas! we are every day worse and worse and grow, like a cow's tail, downward. And why all this? We have a Clerk of the Market

not worth three figs, and values more the getting of a penny himself, than any of our lives. 'Tis this makes him laugh in his sleeve, for he gets more money in a day than many an honest man's whole estate. I know very well how he got the fortune he has, but if we were men he would not hug himself as he does. But now the people are grown to this pass, that they are lions at home and foxes abroad. For my part, I have eaten up my clothes already, and if corn holds at the rate it does, I shall be forced to sell house and all. For what will become of us, if neither Gods nor men have mercy on us? Let me never enjoy my friends more, if I don't believe all this comes from heaven. For no body believes in the Gods, no one keeps a fast, or values Jupiter of a hair, but falls on his knees to reckon what he is worth. Time was when our Matrons went in procession up to the Temple, their

feet bare, their hair disheveled, their minds pure, and prayed Jove to send rain. And forthwith it rained pitcherfulls—or then or never—and everybody was in a good humour. Now we have no more reverence for the Gods than for so many mice, so they have grown gouty, and by reason of our irreligion and profaneness our lands and meadows languish—"

"More civilly, I beseech you!" said Echion the quiltmaker. "The worse luck now, the better another time! as said the clown when he lost his brindled hog. What falls not out to-day may happen to-morrow—'tis the way of the world! There is no better country than ours, had it some men in it—though at present it labours under difficulties, and 'tis not alone in that. We must not be so nice; Heaven is equally distant everywhere. Were you in another place, you'd say hogs walked here ready dressed. And now I think on't we shall have an excellent show these holydays, three days of gladiators, not slaves bought for that purpose, but most of them freemen. Our patron Titus has a large soul, a true hot-head, and cares not a straw which side gets the better. I think I should know him, for I belong to him; he's of a right breed both by father and mother, no mongrel. They are well provided with weapons and will fight it out to the last; the theatre will look like a butcher's shambles. And he has wherewithal to do it. His father left him a vast sum, and let him make ducks and drakes with it never so much; the estate will bear it, and he always carries the reputation of it. He has a number of bravoes, a woman charioteer, and Glyco's steward, who was caught amusing his mistress. What a bustle's here between cuckolds and cuckold-makers! But this Glyco, a pennyworth of a man, condemned his steward to the beasts, and what was that but to expose himself? Where lay the servant's crime, who was obliged to do what he did? She rather, that piss-pot, deserved to be tossed by the bull, but he that cannot come at the breech thrashes at the pack-saddle. Yet how could Glyco expect Hermogenes' daughter should make a good end? He could more easily have skinned a flint; a snake hatches no halters. Glyco, Glyco has done for himself; it will be a brand on him as long as he lives nor can anything but hell blot it out. However, every man is his own worst enemy.

"I have now smelled out what entertainment Mammea

is like to give us; he'll be at twopence charges for me and
my company. Which if he does, he will put Norbanus
clean out of favour, for you know he can only win by
coming in on the crest of the wave. And in truth, what
good has he ever done us? He gave us a company of
pitiful gladiators, so old and decrepid, that had you
blown on them they'd have fallen flat on their faces; I
have seen many a better at funeral shows. He slew some
pottery horsemen; you'd have taken them for dunghill
cocks fighting in the dark; one was just a pack mule,
another crump-footed, and a third half dead and ham-
strung into the bargain. There was only one of them, a
Thracian, that made a figure, and even he fought ac-
cording to the book. But upon the whole matter all of
them were well whipped, and what they got from the
rabble was 'Lay it on!' Just a downright running away.
'And yet,' says he, 'I gave you a show'—well, I clapped
among the rest for company. Cast up the account, I gave
more than I received. One good turn requires another!

"You, Agamemnon, seem to be saying: 'What
would that troublesome fellow be at?' You that can
speak, yet do not, you are not of our form and therefore
ridicule what poor men say. We all know that study has
turned your head. Where lies the matter then? Let me
persuade you some day to take a walk in the country and
see our cottage; you'll find there somewhat to eat, a
chicken, some eggs, or the like. Good enough, though
the bad weather had like to have broke us all; yet we'll
find enough to fill our bellies. Your scholar, my little

Cicero, is mightily improved, and if he lives you'll have
a pupil after your own heart. He's pretty forward al-
ready, and whatever spare time he has he spends it at
his book. He's a witty lad and there's good stuff in him,
though he is mad after birds. I killed three of his linnets
the other day and told him the weasels had eaten them,
yet he found other things to play with, and has a pretty
knack at painting. He has now kicked off the Greeks
and shows a good inclination for Latin, though the mas-
ter he has now humours himself in this and cannot be
kept to one thing. He is a mighty scholar, but will not
take pains. There is also another of this sort, not much
troubled with learning, but very diligent, and teaches
more than he knows himself. He comes to our house on
holydays and whatever you give him he's contented. I
therefore bought the boy some law books, for I would
have him get a taste of law for the use of the household.
It can keep the wolf from the door. For he has learning
enough already. Should he balk at it, I design him for
a trade—a barber, a cryer, or at very least a lawyer—
which nothing but the devil can take from him. How
oft have I told him: 'Thou art, sirrah, my first begotten,
and—believe thy father—whatever thou learnest, 'tis all
thy own. See there Phileros the lawyer, had he not
been a scholar he might have starved. It was but yester-
day that he was peddling from door to door with a pack
on his back, and to-day he dares shout down Norbanus.
Letters are a treasure, and a trade never dies.' "

Thus or the like, we were bandying it about, when

Trimalchio returned, and having wiped his face with ointment and washed his hands, he said at once: "Pardon me, my friends, I have been costive for several days and my physicians were to seek about the matter when a suppository of pomegranate wine with turpentine and vinegar relieved me. And now I hope my belly may be ashamed if it keep no better order. For sometimes I have such a rumbling in my guts you'd think an ox bellowed. And therefore if any of you has a mind to ease himself, he need not blush for the matter. There's not one of us born solid. And I think no torment greater than wanting the benefit of going to stool, which is the only thing even Jupiter himself cannot prevent. And do you laugh, Fortunata? you, that break me so often of my sleep by nights. I never denied any man to do that in my room might pleasure himself, and physicians will not allow us to keep anything in our bodies longer than needs must. Therefore, if you have any further occasion, everything is ready in the next room: water, chamber-pots, close-stools, or whatever else may be needful. Believe me, this being hard bound, if it get into the head, disturbs the whole body. I have known many a man lost by it, when they have been so modest to themselves as not to tell what they ailed."

We thanked him for his frankness and the liberty he gave us, and to suppress our laughter set the glass about again; nor did we know that in the midst of such dainties, we were, as they say, to clamber another hill. For upon the flourish of music, the cloth being taken away,

there were brought in three white hogs with collars and bells about their necks, and he that had the charge of them told us the one was two years old, the other three, and the third full grown. I took it at first to have been a company of tumblers, and that the hogs, as the manner is at fairs, were to have shown us some tricks, till Trimalchio, breaking my expectation: "Which of them," said he, "will you have for supper? For cocks, pheasants, and the like trifles are but country fare; but my cooks have coppers will boil a calf whole." And therewith commanding a cook to be called for, he prevented our choice by ordering him to kill the largest, and with a loud voice asked him of what rank of servants in that house he was, to which he answering "of the fortieth." "Were you bought," said the other, "or born in my house?" "Neither," said the cook, "but left you by Pansa's testament." "See then," said Trimalchio, "that you dress it as it should be, or I'll degrade you to running footman."

On which the cook, being thus sensible of his power, went into the kitchen to mind his charge.

But Trimalchio, turning to us with a pleasanter look, asked if the wine pleased us. "If not," said he, "I'll have it changed, and if it does, let me see it by your drinking. I thank the Gods I do not buy it, but have everything that may get an appetite growing on an estate of mine that I as yet have not seen. They tell me it goes from Tarracina to Tarentum. I have a project to join Sicily to my lands on the continent, that when I have a mind to go to Africa I may sail through my own estates.

"But prithee, Agamemnon, tell me what moot point was it you argued to-day? For though I plead no causes myself, yet I have had a share of letters in my time; and that you may not think me sick of them now, I have two libraries, one Greek, the other Latin. Therefore, as you love me, tell me the state of the question." Agamemnon began: "A poor man and a rich man were enemies . . ." and Trimalchio said, "What is a poor man?" "Spoke like a gentleman," replied Agamemnon, and went on to expound I know not what moot point. "If it be so," said Trimalchio, "where lies the dispute? And if it be not so, 'tis nothing."

While we all hummed this and the like stuff, "I beseech you," said he, "my dear Agamemnon, do you remember the twelve labours of Hercules, or the story of Ulysses, how a Cyclops put his thumb out of joint with a claw hammer? I read such things in Homer when I was a boy; nay, saw myself the Sybil of Cuma hanging in a glass bottle, and when the boys asked her, 'Sybil, what wouldst thou?' she answered, 'I would die.'"

He had not yet run to the end of the rope, when an overgrown hog was brought to the table. We all wondered at the quickness of the thing, and swore a capon could not be dressed in the time; and that the more, because the hog seemed larger than was the boar we had just seen. When Trimalchio, looking more intent upon him, "What! what!" said he, "are not his guts taken out? No, by Hercules, they are not! Bring hither, bring hither, this rogue of a cook!" And when the fellow stood hanging his head before us, excusing himself that he was in so much haste he forgot it, "How! Forgot it!" cried out Trimalchio. "You'd think he'd forgotten but the seasoning of pepper and cummin! Strip him!" When in a trice it was done, and himself set between two executioners, we all of us began to intercede for him, as a fault that might now and then happen, and therefore begged his pardon; but if ever he did the like again, there was nobody would speak for him. I, for my part, thought he deserved what he got, and so, turning to Agamemnon's ear, "This fellow," said I, "must be reckoned a careless rascal. Could anyone forget to bowel a hog? I would not, by Hercules, have forgiven him if he had served me so in the dressing of a mackerel!" But Trimalchio, it seems, had somewhat else in his head, for falling a laughing, "You," said he, "that have so short a memory, let's see if you can do it now!" On which the cook, having put on his coat again, took up a knife and, pretending to tremble, ripped up the hog's belly long and thwart, when immediately its own weight tumbled out a heap of hog's-puddings and sausages.

After this, as it had been done of itself, the family gave a shout, and cried out, "Health and prosperity to Caius!" The cook also was presented with wine, a silver coronet, and a drinking bowl on a broad Corinthian plate. Which Agamemnon more narrowly viewing, "I am," said Trimalchio, "the only person that has the true Corinthian vessels." I expected that, according to his usual insolence, he would have told us they had been brought him from Corinth. But he better: "And perhaps," said he, "you'll ask me why I am the only person that have them. And why, but the copper-smith from whom I buy them is called Corinthus? And what is Corinthian, but what is made by Corinthus? But that you may not take me for a man of no sense, I understand well enough whence the word first came. When Troy was taken, Hannibal, a cunning fellow but withal mischievous, made a pile of all the brazen, gold, and silver statues and burnt them together, and thence came this mixed metal, which workmen afterwards carried off and of this mass made platters, dishes and ornaments. So that these vessels are neither this nor that metal, but made of all of them. Pardon me what I say: I had rather have glass ware, at least it stinks not. If glass was not so brittle, I'd reckon it before gold, but now it is of no esteem.

"There was a copper-smith who made glass vessels so tough and hard that they were no more to be broken than gold and silver ones. It so happened that, having made a very fine glass mug fit for no man, as he thought, less than Caesar himself, he went with his present to the Emperor and had admittance. The kind of the gift was praised, the hand of the workman commended, and the design of the giver accepted. He again, that he might turn the admiration of the beholders into astonishment and work himself the more into the Emperor's favour, prayed the glass out of the Emperor's hand; and having received it, threw it with such a force against the paved floor that the most solid and firmest metal could not but have received some hurt thereby. Caesar also was equally troubled and amazed at the action, but the other took up the mug from the ground, not broken, but only a little bulged as if the substance of metal had put on the likeness of glass; and therewith taking a hammer out of his pocket, he hammered it as if it had been a brass kettle and beat out the bruise. And now the fellow thought himself in heaven, having, as he fancied, gotten the acquaintance of Caesar and the admiration of all. But it fell out quite contrary: Caesar asking him if anyone knew how to make this malleable glass but himself. And he answering there was not, the Emperor commanded his head to be struck off. 'For,' said he, 'if this art were once known, gold and silver will be of no more esteem than dirt.'

"As for silver, I more than ordinarily affect it. I have a hundred water-pots more or less, whereon is the story how Cassandra killed her sons, and the dead boys are so well embossed you'd think them alive. I have also a drinking cup left me by a patron of mine, where Daedalus puts Niobe into the Trojan horse, and I have all the fights of Hermeros and Petraites embossed on cups, and all massy plate. Nor will I part with my understanding of them at any rate."

While he was thus talking, a cup dropped out of a boy's hand, on which Trimalchio, looking over his shoulder at him, bade him begone and whip himself immediately, "for," said he, "thou art careless and mindst not what thou art about!" The boy hung his lip and besought him; but he said, "What! dost thou beseech me, as if I required some difficult matter of thee? I only bid thee obtain this of thyself, that thou be not careless again." But at last he discharged him upon our entreaty. On this the boy run round the table and cried, "Water without doors, and wine within!" We all took the jest, and especially Agamemnon, who knew on what account he had been invited hither.

Trimalchio, in the meantime, hearing himself commended, drank all the merrier, and being within an ace of quite out, "Will none of you," said he, "desire my Fortunata to dance? Believe me, there's no one leads up a country dance better." And with that, tossing his hands round his head, he began to act the part of a Jack-Pudding, the family all the while singing: "Youth itself, most exactly, Youth itself!" And he had gotten into the middle of the room, but that Fortunata whispered him and, I believe, told him such gambols did not become his gravity. Nor was there anything more unsteady than his humour, for one while he inclined to the advice of Fortunata and another while to his natural inclination.

But what disturbed the pleasure of his dancing was his notary's coming in, who, as they had been acts of a Common Council, read aloud:

"The Seventh of the Kalends of August: born in Trimalchio's Manor at Cumae, thirty boys and forty girls. Brought from the threshing-floor into the granary, five hundred thousand bushels of wheat.

"The same day: the slave Mithridates was crucified, for having cursed the genius of our Caius.

"The same day: broke out a fire in a pleasure-garden that was Pompey's, which first began in the house of Nasta the bailiff."

"How's this?" said Trimalchio, "When were those gardens bought for me?" "The year before," answered the notary, "and therefore not yet brought to account."

At this Trimalchio fell into a passion, and "Whatever lands," said he, "shall be bought me hereafter, if I hear nothing of it in six months, let them never, I order you, be charged or brought to any account of mine." Then also were read the orders of the Clerks of the Market, and the wills of his foresters, rangers and park keepers, in which they amply praised Trimalchio for letting them disinherit him. Next that, were recited the names of his bailiffs; and how one of the rangers turned off his wife for having taken her in bed with a bath attendant; a door-keeper turned out of office and exiled to Baiae; an

auditor found short in his accounts and tried before the council of the grooms of the bedchamber.

At last came in the dancers on the rope; and a punch-bellied blockhead standing out with a ladder commanded his boy to hop upon every round of it singing, and dance a jig on the top, and then tumble through burning hoops, holding a ewer by his teeth. Trimalchio was the only person that liked this diversion and called it a thankless task, and withal he said there were but two things he could willingly behold, the fliers on the high rope and the trumpeters, and that all other creatures and shows were mere trifles. "For," said he, "I bought once a set of strollers, and chose rather to make them merry-andrews than comedians, and commanded my bag-piper to sing in Latin to them."

While he was chattering at this rate, the boy chanced to fall on him, on which the family gave a shriek; the same also did the guests, not for such a beast of a man, whose neck they could willingly have seen broken, but for fear the supper should break up ill, and they be forced to wail the death of a stranger.

Whatever it were, Trimalchio gave a deep groan and leaning upon his arm as if it had been hurt, the physicians ran thick about him, and with the first, Fortunata, her hair about her ears, a bottle of wine in her hand, still howling, miserable unfortunate woman she was! Undone! She was undone!

The boy, on the other hand, ran under our feet and beseeched us to procure him his pardon. But I was much concerned lest our interposition might turn the matter into a scurvy jest, for the cook that had forgotten to disbowel the hog was still in my thoughts. I began, therefore, to look about the room for fear somewhat or other might drop through the ceiling, while the servant that had bound up his arm in white, not scarlet coloured flannel, was soundly beaten. Nor was I much out, for instead of a punishment there came an order of Trimalchio's by which he gave the boy his freedom, that it might not be said so honourable a person had been hurt by a slave.

We all commended the action, and from thence fell into a chat of the instability of all human affairs. "You're in the right," said Trimalchio, "nor ought this accident to pass without recording." And so, calling for his journal, he commanded it to be entered, and presently, without much thinking, tumbled out these verses:

petronius

What's least expected falls into our dish,
And fortune's more indulgent than our wish:
Therefore, boy, fill the generous wine about.

This epigram gave us occasion to talk of the poets
... and Mopsus, the Thracian, was a long while thought
most deserving of the bays, till Trimalchio, "I beseech
you, Professor," said he, "what difference take you be-
tween Cicero the orator and Publilius the poet? For my
part I think one the more eloquent, the other the prettier
man; for what could be said better than this:

Now sinking Rome grows weak with luxury,
To please her appetite crammed peacocks die
Whose gaudy plumes a modish dish supply.
For her the guinea-hen and capon's dressed;
The stork itself for Rome's luxurious taste
Must in a cauldron build its humble nest:
That foreign, friendly, pious, long-legged thing,
Grateful, that with shrill sounding notes does sing
All winter's gone, yet ushers in the spring.
Why in one ring must three rich pearls be worn,
But that your wives the exhausted seas adorn,
Abroad t'ncrease their lust, at home their scorn?
Why is the costly emerald so desired
Or richer glittering carbuncle admired?
Because they sparkle? is't with that you're fired?
Well, honesty's a jewel. Now none knows
A modest bride from a kept whore by 'er clothes,
For cobweb lawns both spouse and wench expose.

"But now we are talking, which, after literature, is it
your opinion is the most difficult trade? I think a physi-

cian and a banker: a physician, because he knows a man's very heart, and when the fits of an ague will return—though, by the way, I hate them mortally, for by their good will I should have nothing but slubber-slops—and a banker, because he'll find out a piece of brass though 'tis plated with silver. There are also brute beasts, sheep and oxen, laborious in their kind: oxen, to whom we are beholden for the bread we eat, and sheep, for the wool that makes us so fine. But, Oh horrid!, we both eat the mutton and make us warm with the fleece. I take the bees for divine creatures; they give us honey, though 'tis said they stole it from Jupiter, and that's the reason why they sting; for wherever you meet anything that's sweet, you'll ever find a sting at the end of it."

And now he was taking their trade from the philosophers, when lottery tickets were carried round the table in an urn, and a boy, set for that purpose, read aloud the names of the presents appointed for the guests to carry home with them: "Leggy silver!"—and in came a gammon of bacon with a silver cruet. "A pillow!"—a brisket was brought in. "Second thoughts and contumely!"—the winner received salt tack and apples. "Pears and peaches!"—a whip and a knife. "Sparrows and fly-flaps!"—raisins and Athenian honey. "Court dress and town dress!"—a pie and table books. "Channel and pedal!"—a hare and slippers. "Lamprey and letter!"—a rat with a frog tied to his tail and a bundle of beets. Long time we laughed at these and five hundred the like that have now slipped my memory.

But now when Ascyltos, who could not moderate himself, held up his hands and laughed at everything so heartily that he was ready to cry, a fellow freedman of Trimalchio's that sat next above me grew hot upon't and, "What," said he, "thou sheep, what do you laugh at! Does not this magnificence of my Lord please you? You're richer than he—forsooth!—and eat better every day! By the God of this place, had I sat near enough you I would have hit you a box on the ear before now! A hopeful scoundrel, that mocks others; some pitiful night-walker, not worth the very urine he makes, and should I throw mine on him, he knows not where to dry himself. I am not, by Hercules, quickly angry, yet worms are bred even in tender flesh! He laughs! what has he to laugh at? What wool did his father give for the bantling? You're a Roman knight? Well then, I am the son of a King. How came I then, say you, to serve another? I did it of myself, and had rather be a citizen of Rome than a tributary King, and now hope to live so as to be no man's jest. I walk like other men with an open face, and can show my head among the best, for I owe no man a groat: I never had an action brought against me, nor can any man say to me on the Exchange: 'Pay me what thou owest!' I have purchased a pretty farm and have some money in the bank; I feed twenty mouths, besides a dog; I ransomed my bond-woman, lest another should wipe his hands on her smock; I paid a thousand for my own freedom; I was elected to the Sevirs' Lodge gratis; and I hope so to die that I shall have no occasion to blush in my grave. But are you so prying into others that you never consider yourself? Can you see a mote in another man's eye and not perceive a beam in your own? Your teacher here, a man ancienter than yourself, we please him; but yet thou, whose milk is not yet out of thy nose, that can'st not say Boh to a goose, must you be making observations? You're the wealthier man? You dine twice and sup twice in a day? For my part I value my credit more than treasures. Upon the whole matter, where's the man that ever dunned me twice? Thou pipkin of a man, more limber but nothing better than a strop of wet leather! I served for forty years, yet none knew whether I was a free man or a slave. I came to this town as a boy with long curls; the Court house had not yet been built. Yet I made it my business to please my master, a person of honour, the parings of whose nails were worth more than thy whole body. I met several rubs in my way but, by the help of my good angel, I broke through them all. These are true feats; for as to being born free it is no harder than saying 'come here.' What makes you in the dumps now, like a goat at a heap of stones?"

On this, Gito, who stood behind him, burst out a laughing, which the other taking notice of, fell upon the boy and, "Do you," said he, "laugh too, you curl-pated, chattering magpie? Are these holidays? Why, how now, sirrah? is it the month of December? When did you count out your freedom tax? What would this collop dropped from the gibbet, this crow's meat, be at? I'll find some way or other for Jupiter to plague thee, and him that taught thee no better manners. Never let me eat a good meal's-meat again, if I do not spare thee for mine host's sake, else I would pay thee in good sound coin. We are all having a pleasant time, but for these cullions who cannot govern thee. For without doubt it is true: like master, like man. I am not hot by nature, yet I can scarce contain myself; when I once break out, I care not two-pence for my mother. Very well, I shall meet thee abroad, thou mouse, nay, rather mole-hill. May I never thrive more this way or that, but I'll drive that master of thine into a blade of rue. Nor shalt thou, by Hercules, get out of my clutches, though thou couldst call in Olympian Jupiter to thy aid. I shall off with those locks not worth a groat, and with that master of thine not worth two. Thou wilt certainly fall into my hands, and either I know not myself or I'll make thee leave this buffoonery, though thy beard were made of gold. I'll have thee bruised in a mortar, and him that first taught thee. I never studied geometry, criticism, and mere words without sense, but I can read print and I know my tables of weights, measures, coin. If you have a mind, you and I will try it between us; I'll lay thee a wager. Come, here's my stake. Thou willst soon learn that thy father wasted his money when he taught thee rhetoric. 'Which of us? I come long, I come wide. Guess me!' Resolve me, I say, 'which of us runs yet stirs not out of his place? Which of us grows bigger and yet is less?' Do you scamper? Can't you tell what to make of it, that you look so like a mouse in a trap? Therefore hold thy tongue and don't provoke a better man than thyself who thinks thee but a scoundrel of nature. Unless thou fanciest me taken with those rings of yellow box-wood which you stole from your mistress. Oh lucky opportunity! Come, let's walk the Exchange and see which of us can take up money; you'll be satisfied then this iron ring has credit upon it. A pretty thing, is it not, a drunken fox! So may I gain while I live and die so well that all the people will swear by my funeral, if I sit not on your skirts as close as the coat to your back. He's a precious tool, too, that taught thee, a piece of green cheese, no master. We learnt otherwise at school; our master used to say: 'Are your things in order? Get you home as fast as you can! Look well about you! Have a care how you speak irreverently of your betters!' But now all this is nonsense and no one is worth two-pence. For myself, I thank God you see me as I am!"

Ascyltos was making answer to his railing, when Trimalchio, pleased with the good grace with which his fellow freedman delivered himself, "Go to," said he, "no more of this wild talk; let us rather be merry. And you, Hermeros, bear with the young man. His blood boils, be thou the soberer man. He that is overcome in this matter, goes off conqueror. Even you yourself, when you were such another capon, could cry nothing but Coco! Coco! and had no heart at all. Let us therefore, which is the better of the two, be heartily merry and watch a masque from Homer."

Nor were the words scarce out of his mouth when in came a company of players and made a rustling with their spears and targets. Trimalchio leaned on his pillow and, while the players rattled out Greek verses as arrogantly as they are wont to do, he read from a Latin book in sing-song. Whereupon silence being made, "Know ye," said he, "the argument of this masque? Diomedes and Ganymedes were two brothers and Helen was their sister; Agamemnon stole her away and shammed Diana with a hind in her place. And Homer says here how the Trojans and the Parentines fought among themselves, but at last he got the better of it and married his daughter Iphigenia to Achilles, on which Ajax went mad. And there's an end of the tale." On this the players set up a shout, the servants ran this way and that, and a boiled calf with a helmet on its head was brought in upon a mighty charger. Ajax followed and, with a drawn sword, as if he were mad, made at it, now in one place then in another, till, having cut it into joints, he took them on the point of his sword and distributed them.

Nor had we much time to admire the conceit, for of a sudden the roof gave a crack and the whole room shook. For my part, I got on my feet, but all in confusion, for fear some tumbler might drop on my head; the same also were the rest of the guests, still gaping and expecting what new thing should come from the clouds, when straight the main beams of the ceiling opened and a vast circle was let down, the hoop no doubt of some huge tun, all round which hung golden garlands and alabaster pots of sweet ointments.

While we were required to take up these presents I chanced to cast an eye upon the table where lay a fresh service of cheese-cakes and tarts, and in the midst of them a baked image of the God which presides over orchards, stuck round with all sorts of apples and grapes, as they commonly draw that figure. We greedily reached our hands toward it, when of a sudden, a new diversion gave us fresh mirth; for all the cheese-cakes, apples and tarts, upon the least touch, threw out delicious liquid saffron, which fell upon us. We, judging the mess to be sacred that was so religiously set out, stood up and began a health "To Augustus, the Father of his Country!" After which reverence, falling to catch that catch could, we filled our napkins, and I more furiously than the rest, who thought nothing too good for my boy Gito.

As these things were doing, in came three boys in white, their coats tucked about them, of whom two set on the table household Gods with lockets about their necks, and the other, bearing round us a goblet of wine, cried aloud, "Be the Gods favourable!" And he said that one was named Good-gain, the second Good-luck, and the third Good-increase. And as the image of Trimalchio was carried round and everyone kissed it, we thought it a shame not to do as the rest of the company.

After this, when all of us had wished each other health and happiness, Trimalchio, turning to Niceros, "You were wont," said he, "to be a good companion, but what's the matter we get not a word from you now? Let me entreat you, if you wish me well, tell us some tale you have at hand!" Niceros, pleased with the frankness of his friend, "Let me never thrive," said he, "if I am not ready to caper out of my skin to see you in so good a humour. Therefore what I say shall be all mirth, though I am afraid these grave scholars may laugh. But let them look to it, I'll go on nevertheless, for what am I the worse for anyone's laughing? I had rather they laugh at what I say than at myself."

When he had thus spoke he began this tale: "While I was yet a slave, we lived in Narrow Lane, now the house of Gavilla. There, as the Gods would have it, I fell in love with the wife of Terentius, the cook. Ye all knew

Melissa of Tarentum, a pretty little punching-block and withal beautiful, but, by Hercules, I mended her not so much for that, as that she was good-humoured. If I asked her for anything she never denied me; and what money I had I trusted her with it, nor did she ever fail me when I had occasion for it. It so happened that her husband died while they were in the country. Therefore I left no stone unturned to find a way to come to her: a friend is seen at a dead lift.

"It also fell out that my master was gone to Capua to dispatch some business. I laid hold of the opportunity and persuaded a guest who was sojourning with us to accompany me as far as the fifth milestone. He was a soldier, as strong as the devil. We made off at cock-crowing; the moon shone as bright as day. We came to the tomb monuments; my man loitered behind me to ease himself against a tombstone. I sat down expecting him and fell to singing and numbering the stars. When looking round me what should I see but my companion stripped stark naked and his clothes lying by the high-way side. My soul was in my mouth and I stood as if I had been dead, but he pissed around his clothes and of a sudden was turned to a wolf. Don't think I jest; I would not tell a lie for any man's estate. But as I was saying, after he was turned to a wolf, he set up a howl and fled to the woods. At first I knew not where I was, till, going to take up his clothes, I found them also turned to stone. Another man would have died for fear, but I drew my sword and, slaying all the shadows that came in my way, lighted at last on the farm where my mistress was. I entered like a ghost, my eyes were sunk in my head, the sweat ran off me by more streams than one, I could hardly believe I should ever recover. When my Melissa coming to me began to wonder why I'd be walking so late, and 'If,' said she, 'you had come a little sooner, you might have done us a kindness, for a wolf came into the farm, and has made butcher's work enough among the cattle. But though he got off, he has no reason to laugh, for a servant of ours ran him through the neck with a pitch-fork.' As soon as I heard her, I could not close an eye, and ran home by daylight like a vintner whose house had been robbed. But coming by the place where the clothes were turned to stone, I saw nothing but a puddle of blood, and when I got home found the fellow lying a-bed like an ox in a stall and a surgeon dressing his neck. I then understood he was a were-wolf, and from that day forward could never eat a bit of bread with him, no, if you'd have killed me. Let others think what they will of it; if I tell you a lie, may my good angels forsake me."

The company were all in a maze when, "Saving what you have said," quoth Trimalchio, "if there be any faith in man, my hair stands on end, because I know Niceros is no trifler. He's sure of what he says and not given to idle talking. Nay, I'll tell ye as horrible a thing myself. But see there, what's that behind the hangings?

"When I was yet a long-haired boy, for even then I lived a pleasant life, it so happened that the minion of our master died. He was, by Hercules, a pearl, a paragon; nay, perfection itself. But when his poor mother lamented him and we also were doing the same, some witches got round the house on a sudden; you'd have taken them for a pack of hounds hunting a hare. We had then in the house a Cappadocian, a tall fellow, stout and hardy, that would not have stepped an inch out of his way for Jupiter himself. He boldly drew his sword and, wrapping his coat about his left arm, leaped out of the house and, as it might be here,—no harm to the thing I touch!—ran a woman clean through. We heard a pitiful groan, but—not to lie—saw none of them. Our champion came in and threw himself on a bed, but all black and blue, as if he had been thrashed with a flail, for it seems some ill hand had touched him. We shut the door and went on with our mourning, but the mother, taking her son in her arms and stroking him, found nothing but a bolster of straw. It had neither heart, entrails nor anything, for the fairies, belike, had stolen him and left a wad of straw instead. Give me credit, I beseech ye; there are women craftier than we are, play their tricks by night, and turn everything topsy-turvy. After this, that tall swinging fellow of ours never came to himself again, but in a few days died, raving mad."

We all wondered, as not doubting what he said and, kissing the table in reverence, desired the Ladies of the Night to keep their places till we returned home from dinner.

And now we thought the lamps looked double and

the whole room seemed quite another thing, when Tri-
malchio again: "I speak to you, Plocamus, won't you
come in for a share? Will you entertain us with noth-
ing? You used to be a pleasant companion, could sing a
song and tell a tale with the best, but, alas! alas! the
sweetmeats are gone!" "My horses," said the other,
"have run away with my coach, ever since I have grown
gouty. When I was a young fellow I sung so long I had
well-nigh brought myself into a consumption. What do
you tell me of dances, tales, or barber shops? Who ever
came near me but one, only Apelles?" and thereupon,
setting his hand to his mouth, whistled out somewhat, I
know not what, which afterwards he swore was Greek.

In the meanwhile, Trimalchio, who was imitating the
trumpeters, looked on his minion whom he called
Croesus. The boy, blear-eyed and with nasty teeth, em-
ployed himself in swathing a little black bitch over-
grown with fat, in green swaddling clouts and set half a
loaf on the table, which she refusing, he crammed
her with it. Whereupon Trimalchio commanded The
Guardian of his House and Family, Scylax, to be
brought. When presently was led in a huge mastiff on
a chain, who, having a hint given him by a scrape of
the porter's foot, lay down before the table. Whereupon
Trimalchio throwing him a manchet, "There's no one
in this house of mine," said he, "loves me better than
this dog." The boy, taking it in dudgeon that Scylax
should be so commended, laid the bitch on the floor and
challenged the dog to have a rubber with him. On this,

Scylax, after the manner of dogs, set up such a hideous barking that it filled the room, and nearly tore to pieces Croesus's Pearly. Nor did the scuffle end here, for a great candlestick being thrown down upon the table, broke all the crystal glasses and threw scalding oil on some of the guests.

Trimalchio, not to seem concerned at the loss, kissed the boy and commanded him to get on his back; nor was it long ere he was a cock-horse and, slapping his master's shoulders and laughing, cried out, "Fool, Fool! and how many of them have we here?"

Trimalchio, thus kept down for a while, commanded a bumper to be filled and given round to the waiters, with this further proviso: "Whosoever refuses it, pour it down his collar. We have been grave a while, let's now be merry!"

After this came junkets and forced meats, the very remembrance of which, if I may be believed, will not yet down with me. For there were several crammed hens given about under the name of thrushes, and goose eggs with caps upon them, which Trimalchio, not without ostentation, pressed us to eat, adding withal that their bones had been taken out. Nor were the words scarce out of his mouth when a beadle rapped at the door, and one in white, with a company of roisters following him, came in upon us. For my part I was not a little surprised and, by his lordliness taking him for the Mayor of the Town and ourselves within his liberties, was getting on my feet. Agamemnon laughed to see me so concerned and bade me sit still; "for," said he, "this Habbinas is a member of the Sevirs' Lodge, a good mason, and he is said to have a special way with him in making tomb monuments."

Recovered again with his words, I kept my seat and wholly fixed my eyes on Habinnas. He came in drunk, lolling on his wife's shoulders, with some garlands about him, his face all trickling down with ointment. He seated himself at the head of the table and incontinently called for wine and water. Trimalchio, pleased with the humour, himself called for a bigger glass and asked him what entertainment he had whence he came. "Everything," said the other, "but your company, for my inclination was here. Though, by Hercules, all was very well. Scissa kept a nine-days funeral feast for his poor little servant whom he enfranchised on his death-bed. It is said he will have trouble with the Exchequer, for the assessors rate the dead boy at fifty thousand. Yet all was done in good order, though every one of us was obliged to pour half his drink on the grave."

"But," said Trimalchio, "what had ye to eat?" "I'll tell ye," quoth Habinnas, "as near as I can, for my memory is so bad that sometimes I forget my own name. However, for the first dish we had a goodly porker garlanded with sausages, and puddings, goose-giblets, lamb-stones, sweetbreads and gizzards round him. There were also beets and household bread of his own baking, which I had rather have than white: it makes a man strong and helps me at stool. The next was a cold tart with excellent warm honey, right Spanish, running upon it. I ate a little of the tart, but stuffed myself with the honey. Round were red pulse and lupines, as many nuts as we wanted, and an apple apiece, of which I took away two in my handkerchief for if I bring home nothing to my little slave, I shall have snubs enough. But this Dame of mine keeps her eye on me. The main course was the haunch of a bear, which Scintilla tasting ere she was aware, had like to have vomited her guts up. I, on the other hand, ate a pound of it or better, for methought it tasted like boar's flesh. And, say I, if a bear eats a man, why may not a man much more eat a bear? To end with, we had cream cheese, wine boiled off to a third part, fried snails, chitterlings, livers, eggs, turnips, mustard, and a shitty-looking custard. But I'm going too far! There were also handed about a basket of sugar cakes, of which some were rude enough to take three fist fulls. For we sent away the gammon of bacon.

"But tell me, Caius, I beseech you, what's the matter that Fortunata sits not among us?" "How come you not to know her?" quoth Trimalchio. "Till she has gotten her plate together and distributed what we leave among the servants, not a sip of anything goes down her throat." "But unless she sits down," replied Habinnas, "I'll be gone!" and was getting up, but that the word being four times given about for her, she came at last in a greenish gown and a cherry coloured stomacher, beneath which might be seen her petticoat and embroidered garters. Then, wiping her hands on her neckcloth, she placed herself on the bed whereon Scintilla, the wife of Habinnas, was, and having given her a kiss told her it was a compliment to her that she was there. At length it came to this, that she took off her fat arms her bracelets and shewed them to Scintilla, which she admiring, she also unbuckled her garters and a hair net which she said was of the finest gold.

Trimalchio observed it and, commanding all to be laid before him, "See!" said he, "what irons our women wear, and what fools our wives make of us! They should weigh six pound and a half, yet I've another made from hoarding small change that weighs ten!" And that he might not be thought to tell a lie, called for his gold scales and commanded them to be weighed. Nor had Scintilla more wit than t'other, for, pulling out of her bosom a golden box, which she called her talisman, she took out of it two large pearl ear-rings, giving them in like manner to Fortunata to view. "See!" quoth she, "what 'tis to have a kind husband! I am sure no woman has better!" "What!" said Habinnas, "You plagued me till I should buy thee these glass beads. Had I a daughter, I'd cut her ears off! Were there no women in the world, everything would be as cheap as dirt. As things are now, we piss warm and drink cold."

Mean time the women perceiving they were touched, fell a twittering and, being got mellow, fell to kissing one another, the one commending the cares of the mistress of the house, t'other complaining of the minion and her husband's neglect. When during this chit-chat Habinnas, stealing behind Fortunata, gave her such a toss on the bed that her heels flew as high as her head, on which she gave a squeak or two, and finding her thighs bare, blushing, ran her head under Scintilla's smock.

This held a while till, Trimalchio calling for another course, the servants took away the tables that were before us and, having brought others, strewed the room with sawdust mixed with vermillion and saffron, and, what I never saw before, ground alabaster. When immediately says Trimalchio: "I could have been contented with those first dishes, but since we have got other tables, you can also have another course. If there be anything worth our having, bring it in!" On which a spruce boy that served us with warm water began to imitate a nightingale, while Trimalchio kept on saying, "Change it!" Another humour was set up. A servant that waited on Habinnas commanded, as I believe, by his master bellowed out:

"Meantime Aeneas had put off to sea . . ."

Nor was there ever a harsher sound yet pierced my ears, for besides his disordered country tone, his pitiful and starveling way of delivery, he so stuffed it with scraps of verses from the pantomimes, that even Virgil then first disrelished me, till at last he was so tired that he could hold no longer. "Can ye believe," said Habinnas, "that this boy has never been to school? But I bred him with the jugglers that follow the fairs, nor has he his fellow, whether he mimics a muleteer or a buffoon. He has a desperate wit; he's a cobbler, a cook, a baker, a jack of all trades, and, but for two faults, were exact to a hair: he's circumcised and snores in his sleep. For that cast of his eye, I value it not, 'tis the look of Venus. And therefore his tongue is ever running and his eye never still. I bought him for three hundred shillings."

On which Scintilla, interrupting him, told him he was not telling all the qualities of the good-for-nothing slave. "He's a pimp," said she, "if not worse; but I'll take care he be branded for that." Trimalchio laughed and "I recognize," said he, "the Cappadocian that never stints himself of anything. And, by Hercules, I commend him for it; 'tis something none will offer on our graves. But, Scintilla, you must not be jealous. Believe me, we know you women too. May I so enjoy the health you wish me, I played at leap-frog so long with her Ladyship that my Lord grew suspicious, and sent me off to the country. But hold, Tongue, and I'll give thee a loaf!"

Hereupon the rascal, as if he had been praised all this while, took out an earthenware lamp from his bosom and for half an hour or better counterfeited the hautboys, Habinnas singing the base to him, and blabbering his underlip with his finger. That done, he went into the middle of the room and, clattering some canes together, one while imitated the bagpipes and danced a jigg to his own music, and another while, with a ragged frock and a whip, aped the humours of a carrier, till Habinnas having called him, first kissed him and then drank to him. "Better and better, Massa!" said he, "I give you a pair of buskins."

Nor had there ever been an end of this trumpery had not the last course been brought in: thrushes of pie crust stuffed with raisins and chestnuts, and after them quinces so stuck with prickles that they looked like hedgehogs. Yet this might have been borne with, if the next dish had not been such that we had rather have starved than touched it. For when it was set upon the table and, as we thought, looked like a good fat goose with fish and all kind of fowl round it, "All you see here," said Trimalchio, "is made of the same substance!"

Like a cunning loon, I straight apprehended what it might be, and turning to Agamemnon, "I marvel," said I, "whether they be all made of wax or at the very least of clay, for at the Saturnalia in Rome myself saw the like imaginary supper!"

Nor had I scarce said it when quoth Trimalchio: "So may I grow in estate, not bulk, as my cook made all this you see out of one hog. There is not an excellenter fellow in the world than himself. He shall, if you please, make you a poll of ling of a sow's tripe, a wood-culver of fat bacon, a turtle of a spring of pork, and a hen of a collar of brawn. And therefore a fancy took me to give him a name suitable to his parts. You must know I call him Daedalus. And because he understands his business, I had chopping knives of the best Bohemian steel brought him from Rome." And with that, calling for them, he turned them over and admiring them offered us the liberty of trying their edge on our lips.

Immediately on this came in two servants, as though they had been quarrelling at the well, for they still had the water jars hanging from their necks. And when Tri-

malchio determined the matter between them, neither of them stood to his sentence, but fell to club-law and broke each other's pots. This drunken presumption put us out of order, yet, casting an eye on the combatants, we saw oysters and scollops falling from the broken pots, and another boy receiving them in a charger which he carried round to the guests. Nor was the cook's ingenuity short of the rest, for he brought us a dish of broiled snails on a silver gridiron, and with a shrill, unpleasant voice sang as he went. I am ashamed to relate what followed, for, what was never heard of till then, some curly-headed boys came in with a silver basin of liquid perfumes and, first binding our legs, ankles and feet with garlands, anointed them with it, and put the rest into the wine vessels and the lamps.

And now Fortunata began to dance and Scintilla's hands clapped faster than her tongue, when says Trimalchio: "Sit down, Philargyrus, I give you leave; and you too, Cario, even though you are a vile Green, and bid Menophila, your concubine, do the like!"

What shall I say more? The family so crowded upon us that we were almost thrust off our beds, and who should be seated above me but the cook who had made a goose of a hog, all stinking of pickle and kitchen stuff. Nor yet content that he sat amongst us, he fell immediately to impersonate Ephesus, the tragic actor, and dare his master to a wager that at the next races the greens would carry off the first prize.

Trimalchio swelled at the challenge. "My friends,"

said he, "even slaves are men, and, however oppressed by ill luck, sucked the same milk ourselves did; and for mine it shall not be long e'er I make them free without prejudice to myself. To be short, I enfranchise all of them by my last will and testament. I give Philargyrus a farm and his concubine; to Cario a tenement free of tax and a bed and its furniture. For I make my dear Fortunata executrix and residuary legatee, whom I recommend to all my friends and publish what I design to have done, to the end that my family may so love me now as if I were dead." All thanked their master for his kindness, and he, forgetting all trifles, called for a copy of his will, which he read from one end to the other, the family all the while sighing and sobbing. Afterwards, turning to Habinnas, "Tell me, my best of friends," said he, "do you go on with my monument as I directed you? I earnestly entreat you that at the feet of my statue you carve me my little bitch, as also garlands and ointments, and all the fights of my favourite gladiator, Petraites, that by your kindness I may live when I am dead. Be sure too that it have a hundred feet as it fronts the highway, and as it looks towards the fields, two hundred. I will also that there be all sorts of fruit trees round my ashes, and vines in great abundance. For it is a gross mistake to furnish houses for the living, and take no care of those we are to abide in for ever. And therefore, in the first place, I will have it engraven:

LET NO HEIR OF MINE
PRETEND TO THIS MONUMENT

"And that I may receive no injury after I am dead, I'll have a codicil annexed to my will, whereby I'll appoint one of my freedmen the keeper of this monument, that the people make not a house-of-office of it. Make me also, I beseech you, on this my monument, ships under full sail, and myself in my robes sitting on the bench with five gold rings on my fingers and scattering moneys among the common people. For you know I once ordered a general feast with two-pence a-piece in money. You shall also, if you think fit, shape me some dining couches, and show also all the people gorging themselves. On my right hand place my Fortunata's statue with a dove in one hand and with the other leading her little dog on a leash; as also my minion, and large wine vessels close corked that the wine don't run out, and yet carve one of them as broken and a boy weeping over it; as also a sun dial in the middle, that whoever comes to see what's the clock may read my name, whether he will or no. And lastly, have a special consideration whether you think this epitaph sufficient enough: Here rests Caius Pompeius Trimalchio, Patron of the learned. He was appointed Sevir without suing for it. He might have been a master of any guild in Rome would he have accepted it. Pious, honest, valiant, he raised himself from little, but left behind him thirty million, nor ever once listened to a philosopher. Farewell to you also."

This said, Trimalchio wept plentifully, Fortunata wept, Habinnas wept, and the whole family set up a cry, as it had been his funeral. Nay, I also whined for company, when says Trimalchio: "Since we know we must die, why don't we live while we may? So let me live myself to see you happy, as, if we plunge ourselves in the bath, we shall not repent it. At my peril be it; I'll lead the way, for this room is grown as hot as an oven." "Say you so," quoth Habinnas, "nor am I afraid to make two days of one!" and therewith got up barefoot and followed Trimalchio.

I, on the other hand, turning to Ascyltos, asked him what he thought of it, for "if I but see the bath I shall swoon away!" "Let's lag behind then," said he, "and whilst they are getting in, we'll slip off in the crowd." The contrivance pleased us, and so Gito leading the way through the portico, we came to the outermost gate where a chained dog bolted on us so furiously that Ascyltos fell into the fishpond. I, who had been frighted at the painted dog, and now gotten as drunk as Ascyltos, while I endeavoured to get hold of him, fell in myself. At last the porter's coming in saved us, for he quieted the dog and drew us out. But Gito, like a sharp rascal, delivered himself, for whatever had been given to him at supper to carry home with him, he threw it to the dog and that mollified him. But when, shivering with cold, we desired the porter to let us out, "You're mistaken," said he, "if you think to go out the same way you came in, for no guest ever did that yet. They come in at one gate and go out at another."

In this sad pickle, what should we do? We found ourselves in a new kind of labyrinth, and we even began to long for a hot bath. So, necessity enforcing us, we prayed him to show us the way to the bath and, Gito having hung out our clothes a drying in the porch, we entered the bath, which was somewhat narrow and sunk into the earth, not unlike a rainwater cistern. In this stood Trimalchio stark naked. Nor could we avoid his filthy vauntings, for he said nothing was better than to bathe without a crowd, and that very place, in times past, had been a bakery. Being weary at length, he sat down and, provoked by the resonance of the bath, set up his drunken throat and fell a murdering some songs of Menecrates, as they that understood him told us. Other guests ran round the cistern with their arms across, and made a clamorous noise with their mouths. Others either tried to take up a ring from the pavement

with their hands bound behind them, or putting one knee to the ground to kiss their great toes backward.

While they thus entertained one another, we went into the hot house that had been heated for Trimalchio, and being now recovered of our drunkenness, were brought into another room where Fortunata had set out a fresh entertainment. Above the lamps I observed some women's gewgaws and little brass statues of anglers. The tables were massy silver, the earthenware double gilt, and a conduit running with wine, when said Trimalchio, "This day, my friends, a slave of mine had his first shave; he's well to pass, a thrifty fellow, and a favourite of mine. Come, let us be merry and we'll sit to it till daylight."

While he was yet speaking, a cock crowed. At which Trimalchio grew disordered, and commanded the wine to be thrown under the table, and sprinkle the lamps with it. Then, changing a ring to his right hand, "It is not for nothing," said he, "this trumpeter has given notice. For either there is a house on fire, or one of the neighbourhood will kill himself. Far from us be it! And therefore whoever brings me this ill prophet, I'll give him a reward."

When immediately a cock was brought in and, Trimalchio commanding to have him dressed, he was torn in pieces by that exquisite cook who a little before had made us fish and fowl of a hog, and put in a stew pan. And while Daedalus was taking a lusty draught, Fortunata ground pepper. After which, Trimalchio, taking some of the banquet, bid the waiters go to supper, and let others supply their places. Whereupon came in another rank of servants, and as the former going cried out, "Farewell, Caius!" those coming in cried out, "Sit thou merry, Caius!"

And here our mirth first began to be disturbed, for, a beautiful boy coming in among those new servants, Trimalchio plucked the boy to him, and did nothing but kiss him over and over. Whereupon Fortunata, to maintain her right, began to rail at Trimalchio, called him pitiful fellow, one that could not bridle his lust, a shame and scandal to all honest women and, at last, a very dog. Trimalchio, on the other hand, all confounded and vexed at her taunts, threw a goblet at her head. She fell a roaring as if she had lost an eye, and clapped both her hands before her face. Scintilla also stood amazed, and covered Fortunata, all trembling as she was, in her bosom, while an officious page also put a cold pitcher to her cheek, on which she leaned and made a lamentable wailing and blubbering. But Trimalchio quite contrary; "For," said he, "what am I the better for this graceless buttock? 'Tis well known I took her out of a bawdy house and made her an honest woman. But now, blown up like a frog, she bespatters herself: a very block, no woman. But who is born in a hovel never dreams of palaces. May my good genius so befriend me, as I'll bring down this seeming saint, but in her actions a whore rampant. And I, poor fool, could have married a fortune of ten millions. You know I don't lie. Agatho, the perfume seller of the heiress next door, took me aside and 'I beg thee,' said he, 'let not thy name run out!' But whilst I am making her fortune and behaving like a gentleman, I have put a thorn in my own foot. But I'll have a care that she seek me in the grave with her nails. And that you may immediately be sensible, Mistress Minx, of what I design to do, I will not, Habinnas, have you put her statue on my monument, that I have no words with her when I am dead. Nay, that she may know I am able to plague her, she shall not so much as kiss me when I die!"

After this rattling, Habinnas entreated him to give over his anger. "There's none of us all," said he, "but some time or other does amiss. We are but men, not Gods." Weeping Scintilla said the same, and called him Caius, and by his own good nature, besought him to be pacified.

Trimalchio not able to hold tears any longer, "I beg of you, Habinnas," said he, "and as you wish to enjoy what you have gotten, if I have done anything without cause, spit in my face. I kissed the boy, 'tis true—not for his beauty, but that he's a hopeful, thrifty lad. He has his tables by heart, can read a book at first sight, saves money out of his day's provision, has a little box of his own to keep it, and two drinking cups; and does he not deserve to be in my favour? But Fortunata, forsooth, will not have it so! Is that what you think, bandy-legs? Be content with your own, thou she-kite, and don't plague me so, thou harlotry, or otherwise thou'lt find out what I am. Thou knowest well enough, if I once set on't, I am immovable.

"But we'll remember the living. Come, my friends, let's see how merry you can be! For in my time I have been no better than yourselves, but by my own industry I am what I am. 'Tis the heart makes a man, all the rest is but stuff. I buy cheap and sell dear; another man may tell you otherwise. But I enjoy myself. But thou, thou snorer, art thou yet gruntling? I'll take care hereafter you whimper for something. But, as I was saying, my frugality made me the man I am. I came out of Asia no taller than this candlestick, and daily measured myself by it; and that I might get a beard the sooner, rubbed my lips with the candle grease. Yet I kept Ganymede to my master fourteen years—nor is any thing dishonourable that the master commands—and the same time satisfied my mistress. You understand me, gentlemen; I'll say no more, for I am no boaster.

"By this means, as the Gods would have it, the government of the house was committed to me and nothing was done but by my guidance. What need many words? My master made me joint-heir with Caesar, and I got by his will a senator's estate. But no man thinks he has enough, and I had a mighty desire to turn merchant. Not to detain you longer: I built five ships, freighted them with wines—which at that time were as dear as gold—and sent them to Rome. You'll think I desired to have it so; all my ships foundered at sea. 'Tis a true story I tell you. Neptune swallowed me in one day thirty million.

Do you think I broke upon't? By Hercules, no! The loss was but a flea-bite. For, as if there had been no such thing, I built others, larger, better, and more fortunate than the former, so that every one called me a man of courage. As you know, a great ship carries a great deal of strength. I loaded them again with wine, bacon, beans, unguents, slaves. And here Fortunata showed her affection; for she sold what she had, her jewels, nay, stripped herself to her very smock, and put a round sum of money in my pocket. 'Twas the yeast that raised my fortune. What the Gods will is quickly done. I cleared ten million by the voyage, and forthwith redeemed the lands my patron had left me, built me a house, bought marketfuls of slaves and cattle. And whatever I went about gathered like a snowball. But when I grew richer than all the country besides, I gave over and from a merchant, turned usurer, and let out money to freedmen. Thus resolved to give over trading, I was confirmed in this opinion by a certain astrologer that chanced to light on this town. He was a Graecian, his name Serapa, one that held correspondence with the Gods. He told me a deal I had forgotten, and laid everything before me from top to bottom. He knew all I had within me, and told me what I had the night before for supper. You'd have thought he had lived with me all his life.

"I beseech you, Habinnas, for I think you was there—he told me I should find a mistress among my possessions, that I had but ill luck at friends, that no one ever

made me a return of my kindnesses, that I nourished a
viper in my bosom. And—why should I not tell you
all?—I have by his account thirty years, four months and
two days to live, and in a short time shall have another
estate left me.

"Thus my fortune teller. But if I can join my lands
here to those in Apulia, I shall do well enough. In the
meantime, by the favour of Mercury, my guardian, I
have built this house. It was once, you know, a pitiful
cabin, but now as magnificent as a temple. It has four
dining-rooms, twenty bed-chambers, two marble porti-
coes, a gallery above stairs, my own apartment, another
for this viper, a very good porter's lodge, and a guest
wing. To be short, whenever Scaurus comes this way,
he had rather lodge here than at his family mansion,
though it borders on the sea. And many other conven-
iences it has, which I'll show you by and by. Believe me,
he that has a penny in his purse is worth a penny; they
that have much shall have more. And so your friend,
once no better than a frog, is now a king. And now,
Stichus, bring me the shroud in which I design to be
carried to my funeral pile. Bring also the unguents and
a taste of that bottle which I ordered for the cleansing
my bones."

Stichus lingered not, and brought in a white shroud
and robe of state, and prayed us to try if they were not
fine wool and well woven. "And see you, Stichus," said
Trimalchio smiling, "that neither mice nor moths come
at them, for if they do I'll burn you alive! I will be

brought out in pomp, that all the people may speak well of me." With that, opening a glass bottle of spikenard, he caused us all to be anointed, and, "I hope," said he, "it will do me as much good when I am dead as it does while I am living." Then, commanding the wine vessels to be filled again, "Now imagine," said he, "you are invited to my funeral feast."

We, by this time nauseated, were ready to vomit; Trimalchio also was gotten confoundedly drunk, when—behold!—a new interlude. He called for the cornets to come in and, lying at his full length upon the bed, with pillows under him, "Suppose me," said he, "now dead. Say somewhat, I beseech you, in praise of me." Whereupon the cornets sounded as at a funeral; but one above the rest, a servant of that undertaker who was the honestest man of them all, made such a thundering that it raised the neighbourhood. On which, the watch, thinking the house was on fire, broke open the gate and, making an uproar after their manner, ran in with water and hatchets. When, finding so fair an opportunity, we gave Agamemnon the slip and scampered off as if it had been a real fire.

THE
Second Part
OF THE WORKS OF
Petronius Arbiter
IN PROSE AND
VERSE

MADE ENGLISH BY MR. BURNABY, MR.
THO. BROWN, CAPT. AYLOFF, AND OTHERS

NOT A STAR APPEARED
to direct us in our way, nor would the dead of the night give us hopes of meeting a stranger that could. Our little knowledge of the town and the wine we had drank conspired to guide us amiss.

When we had wandered almost an hour, with our feet all bloody, over sharp pebbles and broken pots, Gito's diligence at last delivered us. For the day before, fearing we might be at a loss, though we had the sun to our help, he had providently marked every post and pillar with a chalk the greatest darkness was not able to obscure, by whose shining whiteness we found our way. Nor were our troubles over after we were got to our inn, for the hostess, having drank a little too long with her guests, had so entirely lost her senses and was fallen into so fast a sleep that throwing her into the fire would scarce have waked her. And perhaps we had been forced to take up our lodgings in the street if a post belonging to Trimalchio, with ten carriages of his master's revenue, had not come in the mean time, who without much ado beat down the door and let us in through the breach.

«As soon as ever we had entered our chamber, having plentifully feasted, pressed by impatient nature, I took my Gito aside and, wrapped in pleasures, spent the night.»

> Who can the charms of that blest night declare,
> How soft—ye Gods!—our warm embraces were!
> We hugged, we clinged, and through each other's lips
> Our souls, like meeting streams, together mixed.
> Farewell the world and all its pageantry!
> When I, a mortal, so begin to die!

But these dreams of satisfaction quickly vanished and I immediately found, to my cost, that I had no reason to hug myself in my pleasures. Ascyltos, naturally prone to mischief, perceiving me drunk and unable to secure my prize, stole the boy out of my bed and conveyed him to his own, and there revelled in joys he had no title to. Gito, either insensible of the change put upon him or cunningly dissembling it, slept, unconcerned at and unmindful of the vows he had made to the contrary. Rising therefore in the morning and finding out the trick imposed upon me, by all that's good, I had a strong inclination to have run them both through together and to have made their sleep eternal by sending them into the other world. But cooler thoughts taking place, I waked my friend Gito with a good drubbing and, looking sternly on Ascyltos, "Since you have played the villain," said I, "and broke the common laws of friendship, pack up your matters quickly and find out another comrade to abuse."

Ascyltos consented and after we had made an exact division of our booty, "Now," says he, "let's share the boy too!" I believed it a jest at parting, but he, with a murderous resolution, drew his sword. "Nor shall you," added he, "think to engross the prize which should, like the rest, be common to us both. I must have my share of him. In case you refuse me I am resolved to take my dividend no other way but with my sword." Upon which I also drew my sword and wrapping my gown about my arm stood ready to engage.

The unhappy boy rushed between and, kissing both our knees with tears, entreated that we would not expose ourselves like Theban brothers in a pitiful alehouse nor with our blood pollute the sacred obligation of so dear a friendship. But raising his voice, says he, "If there must be murder, behold my naked bosom! Hither di-

rect your fury! 'Tis I deserve death, who violated the vows of friendship!" Upon which we sheathed our swords, and first Ascyltos, "I'll end," says he, "the difference. Let the boy himself follow whom he pleases, provided he enjoy perfect liberty in the choice of his friend." I, that presumed so long an acquaintance had made no slight impressions on his nature, was so far from fearing anything that with an eager haste I catched at the proposal and to the judge committed the dispute. But scarce had I finished speaking than Gito jumped up and, without the least hesitation, chose Ascyltos.

I, like one thunderstruck at the sentence, void of defence, fell flat upon the bed, nor had I survived the loss if envy of my rival had not stopped my sword. Ascyltos, proud of the conquest, goes off with the prize leaving me exposed to the insults of Fortune whom a little before he had caressed as a friend and partner of his adventures.

> 'Tis in the world as in a game of chess
> We serve our friends but where our profit is.
> When fortune smiles we're yours, and yours alone,
> But when she frowns the servile herd are gone.
> So in a play, they act with mimic art
> Father or son or griping miser's part:
> But when at last the comic scene is o'er
> They quit the visards they assumed before.

I durst not indulge my grief any longer in that place, for fear, amongst the rest of my misfortunes, that Menelaus the schoolmaster might find me alone in the inn. I therefore tied up my knapsack and, very pensive, took me a lodging in a retired place by the sea. There, after I had been mewed up for three days, reflecting afresh on my despised and abject condition, I beat my breast as sick as it was, and when my deep sighs would suffer me, often cried out: "Why has not the earth burst open and swallowed me alive? Why has not the sea overwhelmed me, that respects not even the innocent themselves? I have fled from justice, I have cheated the gallows, I have slain mine host, but to what purpose? After such daring deeds, to lie alone, a beggar and an exile, in the inn of a Greek town! And who condemned me to this solitude? A boy! A prostitute to all manner of lust, who by his own confession deserves to die, whom vice has ennobled from a slave, who was married as a girl, by one that knew he was of the other sex! And what a wretch is that other, ye Gods! Who no sooner arrived at being a man, but persuaded by his mother he changed himself into a woman and, putting on petticoats, was condemned to a maid's office in a prison; who having spent what he had and changed the scene of his lust, having contracted an old friendship, basely left it and—O horrid impudence! —like a hot whore, for one night's poor pleasure sold his friend! Now the lovers lie whole nights locked in each other's arms and, who knows but in those intervals when they recruit their wearied strength, may laugh at me and the solitude I am in. But they shan't go off so, for as I am a man, free born and generously bred, I'll make their blood expiate the injury!"

Having thus said, I girt on my sword and, lest I should be too weak to maintain the war, encouraged myself with a lusty meal and, making out of doors like one possessed, searched every place. But whilst with a wild distracted countenance I thought of nothing but blood and slaughter and oft with execrations laid my hand on my sword, a soldier, or perhaps some sharper or foot-pad, observed me and, making up to me, said, "Brother soldier, to what regiment or company do you belong?" With a good deal of impudence I named him both the Battalion and Company in which I pretended to serve, when, looking down, "But friend," said he, "do the soldiers of your company walk about in slippers?" I began to look guilty and by my trembling discovered the lie I had told him, upon which he made me lay down my arms and bid me take care of myself. Thus, robbed of both my weapons and revenge, I returned to my lodging where by degrees, my rage abating, I began in my mind to thank the robber.

> Unhappy Tantalus, amidst the flood
> Where floating apples on the surface stood,
> Ever pursued them with a longing eye,
> Yet could not thirst nor hunger satisfy.
> Such is the miser's fate who, cursed with wealth,
> In midst of endless treasure starves himself.

«But finding it difficult to wean myself from the love of revenge, I spent half the night very pensively and, rising by daybreak, to ease me of my grief and thoughts of my injury, I roved about everywhere» till at last I

came to a public gallery, very wonderful for several sorts of excellent paintings. I saw some pieces by Zeuxis' hand that had not yet yielded to the injuries of time and not without an awful reverence, considered others done by Protogenes which, though they were his first trials, yet disputed for exactness even with nature herself. But on the other side viewing a celebrated piece of Apelles I even adored the work of so great a master; 'twas so correctly finished and so much to the life you'd have sworn it a picture of the soul too. One picture gave the story of the eagle bearing the boy of Ida high into heaven, another the fair Hylas repelling the addresses of the lewd naiad. In a third was Apollo angry with himself for killing his boy Hyacinth and to show his love crowned his harp with the flower that sprung from his blood.

Amongst all these painted lovers yet thinking myself alone I burst out: "So the Gods themselves are not secure from love! Jupiter in his heavenly seraglio, not finding one that can please his appetite, sins upon earth, yet injures nobody. The nymph would have stifled her passion for Hylas had she believed the lusty Hercules would have forbid the banns, and all myths made every deity enjoy his wishes without a rival. But I have caressed as the dearest friend the greatest villain!"

While I was thus talking to myself, there entered the gallery an old man with a face as pale as age had made his hair, and seemed, I know not how, to bring with him the air of a great soul; but viewing his contemptible dress and habit, by that very token I immediately con-

cluded him in the number of learned men to whom rich
men have a mortal aversion. In short, he made up to me
and, addressing himself, told me he was a poet and, as
he hoped, one above the common herd; "If my merit,"
added he, "don't suffer by that applause that's promiscu-
ously given to the good and bad." "Why, therefore,"
interrupted I, "are you so meanly clad?" "On this ac-
count," returned he, "because learning never made any
man rich.

> The merchant's profit well rewards his toil:
> The soldier crowns his labours with the spoil:
> To servile flattery we altars raise,
> And the kind wife her stallion ever pays.
> But starving wit in rags takes barren pain
> And, dying, seeks the Muses' aid in vain.

" 'Tis certain," added he, "that a lover of virtue, on
account of his singularity, meets with contempt, for who
can approve what is different from himself? And that
those that admire riches would fain possess everybody,
nothing is more reasonable than their opinion. Whence
they ridicule as well as they can the learned few, that
they, like themselves, might seem within the power of
money." "I don't know how learning and poverty be-
came relations," «said I, and sighed. "You justly la-
ment," said he, "the condition of scholars." "You mis-
take me," said I, "that's not the occasion for my sighs;
there's another and much greater cause." And as all men
are naturally inclined to communicate their grief, I laid
open my case to him, beginning with Ascyltos' treach-

ery, which I aggravated, and with repeated sighs» wished the enemy who had imposed such continence on me might relent, but now he was a hardened villain and in lust more subtle than a carted bawd. «The old man, believing me sincere, began to comfort me and, the better to effect it, told me what formerly had happened to himself on the like occasion:»

"When I was in Asia as a hired clerk in the Treasury Office I took lodgings in a house in Pergamon, attracted not only by the neatness of the apartment but also by the great beauty of the son of the master of the house. My contrivance was to become his lover unsuspected by the father and to effect my wishes I used this method: Whenever at the table we happened to discourse on the use of beautiful boys, I dissembled such a horror of it and pretended my modesty suffered so much by the recital of such gallantries that the mother, in particular, looked upon me as a philosopher above the sensual pleasures of the world. Upon this I was desired to be tutor to the boy, not only to instruct him in a method of study, but also to inform his mind with principles of honour and virtue and to protect his body from any marauder.

"It happened that a festival had cut short his studies and we were lying in the dining room when, about midnight, the long banquet having made us reluctant to go to our rooms, I perceived that the boy was awake. And in timorous whispers I expressed my vow: 'My Lady Venus,' said I, 'could I have the happiness to kiss this boy, and he not know it, to-morrow I'll present him with a pair of turtle doves.' Hearing the reward, the boy began to snore, upon which I greedily seized my wishes. Satisfied with this beginning, I stopped there and early the next morning performed my promise.

"The following night offering the same opportunity, I increased my vow: 'Could I but fondle this boy with lustful hand, and he not know it, I'll present him with a brace of fighting game-cocks.' Hearing this vow, the boy moved closer, fearful, I warrant, lest I should fall asleep. I hastened to calm his fears and enjoyed his body to the full though this side complete pleasure. The next morning I brought him what I had promised.

"When the third night again allowed me I approached the ear of the feigned sleeper and whispered: 'Ye Gods! Could I now obtain from this sleeper the full accomplishment of my desires, for such delight I will give him a fine Macedonian pony, always with the proviso that he not know it!' Never had the boy slept more profoundly, and so I first filled my hands with his milky breasts, next I glued my lips to his, and at last, at one blow, accomplished all my desires.

"On the morrow he sat in his room and awaited the fulfillment of my promise. Now you know how much easier it is to buy doves or game-cocks than a pony and, moreover, so great a gift, I feared, might cause my benevolence to be suspect. And therefore after walking around for some hours I returned home and just kissed the boy. He, throwing his arms round my neck and looking around with care, said, 'I beseech you, sir, where is the pony?'

"This breach of my word should have put a stop to our commerce but I was soon able to resume it. A few days after, a like occasion giving me the like opportunity, when I heard the father snore, I begged him to be friends with me again, that is, to permit himself to be satisfied, and used all the arguments that are prompted by excited lust. But he still sulked and answered nothing but: 'Either you sleep or I'll call father!' But love forces a way through all difficulties; as he was saying 'I'll call father,' I closed in and, meeting with but faint resistance, seized the joy I longed for. He was not displeased with my attempt and after a long complaint that he was cheated, laughed at and abused among his play-fellows whom he had possessed with an opinion of my being very rich, 'to show you,' added he, 'that you shan't meet with the same ingratitude from me, if you have inclinations to repeat your wishes do it freely!' I, laying aside all quarrels, was easily friends with him again and, having used the liberty he gave me, fell fast asleep on the bed. But he that was now in his prime and fit for action was not satisfied and, rousing me, asked, 'Would you have any more?' It was yet no troublesome province to me and when his panting and sweating confessed him satisfied I fell asleep again, exhausted with pleasure. But 'twas hardly an hour ere he was pushing me with his elbow and crying, 'Why not again?' Then I flew into a great passion to be so often disturbed, and turned his own words upon him, 'Either you go to sleep or I'll call your father!' "

This discourse diverting my grief I began to question the old gentleman about the antiquity of some pieces and the stories of others I was not acquainted with, the reason why this age don't come up to the former, and why the most excellent arts are lost, of which painting, in particular, has not left the least sign of its former being.

"Our love of riches," said he, "has been the only occasion. For in old time, when virtue was admired for its own sake, all liberal arts flourished and the only emulation among men was to make discoveries that might profit future ages. 'Twas in those times Democritus found out the virtue of most herbs and, lest there might be any hidden excellence in stones or shrubs, spent the rest of his life in experiments about them. 'Twas then Eudoxus abandoned the world to live on the top of a high mountain and discover the motions of the heavens, and Chrysippus, the better to qualify himself for invention, went thrice through a course of physic. But to return to imagery: Lysippus with such diligence employed himself about one statue that, neglecting his living, he died for want, and Myron, whose brazen images of men and beasts you might have mistaken for living ones, died very poor. But our age is so wholly devoted to drinking and whoring that we are so far from inventing that we even refuse to study those arts which are already found out to our hands. All the business of our schools is to fall foul upon the ancients and we but teach and learn vice only. What's our logic? How little do we know of astronomy? Where's our philosophy? Who now comes to church to pray for eloquence or to drink from the spring of philosophy? They seek not wisdom, health, or moderation, but as soon as they touch the threshold of the Capitol, one promises the Gods a sacrifice should a rich relative be carried off, another if they direct him to a treasure, a third if he should come safely to an estate of thirty million. The very Senate, that should show an exemplary conduct, constantly offers a thousand pounds of gold to the Capitol and tempts Jupiter himself with a bribe, that no one need scruple to wish for money. You need not wonder why painting is lost, when gold appears more beautiful both to Gods and men than anything those poor Greeks, Apelles and Phidias, madly fooled away their time about.

"But, seeing your curiosity is wholly taken up with that piece that shows you the Sack of Troy, I'll try to give you the story more at large in verse.

> Now Troy had felt a siege of ten long years:
> Concern and sorrow on each face appears.
> Calchas the prophet too, with terror filled,
> What fate decreed but doubtfully revealed.
> When thus Apollo, wise Latona's son,
> Shewed them how Troy might by surprise be won:
> 'From the proud top of Ida's rising hill
> A lofty pile of mighty cedars fell,
> Whose trunks into a dreadful fabric force

And let it bear the figure of a horse,
In the great hollows of whose mountain womb
The choice and flower of all your troops entomb.'
The Greeks, enraged to be so long repelled,
With their chief troops the beast's vast bowels filled
And thus their arms and all their troops concealed.
Strange was the fate that ruled unhappy Troy,
Who since they'd gone should lasting peace enjoy.
So the inscription of the machine said
And treacherous Sinon for their ruin made.
All from their arms as from their troubles run
To view the horse and left th' unguarded town.
So overjoyed they wept. Thus even fears,
When joy surprises, melt away in tears.
Enraged Laocoon with prophetic heat
Pressed through the crowds that his wise humour greet,
And with a javelin pierced the fatal horse,
But fate retards the blow and stopped its force.
The spear jumped back against the priest so nigh
It gave new credit to the treachery.
Again his aged strength he vainly tried
And thrust an axe into the wooden side.
Then from within the captive Grecians groan
And at their fear the wooden horse doth moan.
So to the town the captives they convey
And a new stratagem does Troy betray.
　　But other monsters now inform our eyes.
What mighty seas from Tenedos arise!
The frighted Neptune seems to seek the shore
With such a noise, with such a dreadful roar,
As when at dead of night a mighty fleet
With thousand oars the marble sea doth beat.
Now far at sea two fiery snakes appear

And o'er the surge their gilded bellies rear.
Like lofty ships on the green waves they glide
And with their breasts the foaming surge divide.
Their thrashing tails give out a dreadful sound,
Their blazing crests inflame the seas around,
The Ocean trembles at their dreadful hiss.
All wonder! Standing in their priestly dress
While holy wreaths their sacred temples bind,
Laocoon's sons were by the snakes entwined.
Their little hands for aid to heaven they rear,
Each for his brother feels a mutual fear.
Both die at last through fear each other should.
The parent shares his children's fate. The good
Laocoon tries to help with feeble hand:
Full-gorged with blood they drag him o'er the sand
Up to the altar where devoted lies
The priest himself, a panting sacrifice.
So with his blood the temple they profane;
Thus, their Gods lost, Troy's ruin first began.
   Now the bright taper of the night appears
Gaily attended with a train of stars,
When midst the Trojans, dead in sleep and wine,
The Grecians execute their dire design;
Then from the opened caverns of the horse,
Like a large flood, rushes their hidden force.
The courser thus when broke his rein he feels
Bounds on the plain and tries his active heels.
They draw their swords and shake their brazen shields
Which cast bright horror on the dusky fields.
Buried in wine some on the Trojans light
And stretch their sleep to one eternal night;
Some others make the Phrygian altars smoke,
And against Troy, Troy's guardian Gods invoke.

When Eumolpus had gone thus far in his poetical harangue the people that were walking in the portico began to fling stones at him. But he, well accustomed to applause of this kind, covered his head and took to his heels. Fearful lest they should have taken me for a poet too, I made after him. When we had reached the shore and well out of stone shot, "I beseech you, sir," said I, "what will you do with this disease of yours? I have hardly been acquainted with you two hours and your entertainment has had more poetry in it than the conversation of a man in his senses. I don't wonder at the people's humour and I think I must fill my pocket with stones that when I perceive you going into your fit I may bleed you in the head with one of 'em!" He turned to me and, "Dear child," said he, "I was not born yesterday! 'Tis confest I seldom appear even upon the stage to recite but the mob treats me after the same manner. But that I may not be at difference with you too, for to-day I'll tie myself up from this humour of poetry." "Well, well," said I, "on that condition I sup with you." Upon which I ordered the master of our poor lodging to get us a supper.

«In the meantime we went to the bagnio where» I saw Gito standing against the wall with towels and rubbing brushes in his hand. His dejected countenance easily convinced me he served on compulsion. So to put to the proof the evidence of my eyes .... He turned to me with a joyful countenance and, "Have pity, brother," said he, "I can speak freely when not surrounded by weapons.

Snatch me from this bloodthirsty robber and punish as cruelly as you will your penitent judge. It will be sufficient solace to my unhappiness to perish at thy will!" I desired him to waive his complaints lest our design should be discovered and leaving Eumolpus, who was versifying in the bath, we made off through a dirty back-entry, as privately as we could, to my lodgings.

Where, shutting the door, I threw my arms about his neck and, though he was all in tears, half-smothered him with kisses. Thus we continued in a mutual silence; Gito's repeated sobs so disturbed him he could not speak. "How unaccountable is it," began I, "to love him that once forsook me! And that in this breast I should feel so great a wound yet have no sign of its being there! What say you now, you who so easily yielded to an alien love? Have I deserved such usage?" After he found I still had love for him he began to look less concerned. . . . "I chose thee as the judge of our love, but now I neither complain nor even design to remember if only I find thee sincere." I could not tell him this without falling into tears. He wiping my face with his cloak, "Encolpius," said he, "I appeal to your memory, whether I left you or you betrayed me? I must confess, and hope you won't blame me for it, when I saw two at daggers-drawing that I ran to the strongest!" I could not but admire his wit and, to convince him of a perfect reconciliation, sealed it with repeated kisses.

'Twas now quite dark and our supper was dishing up when Eumolpus knocked at the door. I asked how many there was of them and took an opportunity through a chink to see whether Ascyltos was with him but, finding him alone, I soon opened the door. He had hardly fixed himself on his couch when, seeing Gito in waiting, he shook his head and, "A very Ganymede!" said he. "Sure Encolpius, you'll have no reason to complain to-day!"

I did not like a beginning which had so much of curiosity, and was afraid I had entertained another Ascyltos. Eumolpus pursuing his humour when the boy filled him a glass, "I had rather," said he, "be in possession of thee than the whole bagnio!" And, greedily drinking it off, added that never in his life had he passed a worse day: "For, to deal freely with you, I narrowly scaped a beating for attempting, when I was in the bath, to deliver my thoughts in verse to the bystanders. And after I was turned out of the bagnio, as I used to be out of the theatre, I searched every place crying as loud as I could 'Encolpius! Encolpius!' A naked youth that had lost his clothes as strongly echoed back to me 'Gito! Gito!' The boys, believing me mad, ridiculed me with their mimicry, but the other was attended with a great concourse of people that with an awful admiration praised the youth. For nature had so largely qualified him for a lover that his body seemed but the skirt of the mighty member it bore. A lusty rogue! I'll warrant he'd maintain the field four and twenty hours! He therefore soon found relief, for some debauched spark, a Roman knight, as was reported, flung his cloak over him and took him home with hopes, I presume, to engross alone so great a prize. But I was so far from meeting such civility that even my own clothes were kept from me till I brought one that knew me to satisfy them in my character. So much more profitable 'tis to improve the body than the mind!"

Whilst Eumolpus was telling his story I often changed countenance, looking glad at the ill fortune of my rival and troubled at his good, yet I did not interrupt him lest he should discover my concern, and when he had done I told him what we had for supper.

«I had hardly given him an account ere our entertainment came in. 'Twas common, homely fare, but very nourishing. Our half-starved doctor attacked it very briskly, but when he had well filled himself began to tell us philosophers were above the world and ridiculed those that condemn everything because 'tis common and only admire those things that are difficult to be had. "These vicious appetites," added he, "that despise what they can cheaply come by,» never taste anything pure but, like sick men, love only those things that are hurtful to them.

> What's soon obtain'd, we nauseously receive,
> All hate the victory that's got with leave.
> We scorn the good our happy isle brings forth,
> But love whatever is of foreign growth:
> Not that the fish that distant waters feed
> Do those excel that in our climate breed;
> But these are cheaply taken, those came far,
> With difficulty got, and cost us dear.
> Thus the kind she, abroad, we admire above
> Th' insipid lump, at home, of lawful love:
> Yet once enjoyed, we strait anew desire,
> And absent pleasures only do admire."

"Is this," said I, interrupting him, "what you promised, that you would not versify any more to-day? I beseech you, sir, at least spare us that never pelted you! For if any of the inn should smell out a poet in our company the whole neighbourhood would be raised and we should die martyrs for that reason. If nothing else will make you pity us, think of the gallery and bath you came from." When I had treated him after this rate the good-natured Gito, correcting me, said I did very ill to rail at a man so much my elder, and having offered a gentleman the courtesy of my table I should not so far forget good breeding to affront him when he came, with many the like expressions, attended with a blush at their delivery that extremely became him. . . .

"Happy the woman," said Eumolpus, "that's blest with such a son! Heaven increase your virtue! So much sense and so much beauty we seldom meet with in any one person. But lest you should think your civility thrown away, you have found a lover for it. I'll make your praises the subject of my verse. I'll be both your tutor and your guardian and follow you everywhere, whether you will or no. Nor can Encolpius think himself injured; he loves another."

Eumolpus was obliged to the soldier that had robbed me of my sword else I had turned the fury upon him I meant for Ascyltos. Gito reading my anger in my countenance, under pretence of fetching water, prudently withdrew and allayed my heat by removing one cause of it. So as my rage abated, "Eumolpus," said I, "I had rather you plagued me with your verses than propose to yourself such hopes. I am very passionate and you are very lustful. Consider how improbable 'tis we should agree. Believe, therefore, I am mad, and humour the frenzy; that is, be gone immediately!" At this Eumolpus was in great confusion and, without asking the occasion of my passion, presently made out of the room. But pulling the door after him, he locked me in when I least suspected it and, stealing the key, ran in pursuit of Gito.

The rage I was in to be so abused put me upon hanging myself and, having tied my belt to the bedstead, committed my neck to the noose, when Eumolpus and Gito came to the door and, entering, prevented my fatal design. Gito's grief growing to a rage he made a great outcry and, thrusting me on the bed, "You're mistaken," said he, "Encolpius, if you fancy it possible for you to die before me. I was first in the design, and had not survived my choice of Ascyltos if I had met with an instrument of death in his lodgings. But had not you come to my relief in the bath I had resolved to throw myself out of the window. And that you may know death is always ready to wait on those that desire it, see me now as you wished me to see you!" Upon which, having snatched a razor from Eumolpus's servant, he cut three or four times at his throat and fell down before us. Frightened at the accident, I cried out and, falling upon him as he reached the ground, with the same weapon endeavoured to follow him. But neither had Gito any appearance of a wound nor did I feel myself hurt. For it happened to be a dull razor, made blunt on purpose to prepare barbers' 'prentices to handle a sharper. Which was the reason Eumolpus did not offer to prevent our mimic deaths nor his man look concerned when the razor was snatched from him.

While this lovers' scene was acting, the inn-keeper came in upon us with the other part of our supper and, viewing the ridiculous posture we were in, "I beseech you, sirs," said he, "are you drunk or have you fled from justice, or both? And, pray, who was going to make a gallows of my bed? What's the meaning of these tricks? By Hercules! To bilk me of my reckoning you intend to run off during the night! But you shall smart for it! I'll soon make you know that this house is no widow's property but belongs to Marcus Mannicius!" "What, you rascal!" cries Eumolpus, "Do you threaten too?" and without more ado, flung his fist in his face. He, drunk from quaffing many toasts with his guests, took up an earthen pitcher and, throwing it at Eumolpus, broke his forehead and immediately ran down stairs. Eumolpus, impatient of revenge, snatching up a great wooden candlestick, made after him and, pouring his blows very thick on the inn-keeper, revenged the injury to his brow with interest. This put the whole house in an uproar and whilst the rest of his guests, that by this time were most of them drunk, ran to see what was the matter I, taking the opportunity to revenge the injury Eumolpus had offered me, locked him out and, having used him as he used me, enjoyed both bed and board without a rival.

In the meantime the scullions and inhabitants of the tenement set upon Eumolpus. One throws at his head a hot spit with the sizzling meat on it, another seized a toasting fork from the meat larder and put himself in martial posture. But especially a blear-eyed old woman with a dirty apron tucked up about her and one wooden shoe on and the other off, lugged a great mastiff by a chain into the field of battle and set him at Eumolpus. But with the wooden candlestick he defended himself against all his enemies.

We saw all through the hole they had made by wrenching the latch from the door. How well I wished him you may easily imagine, but Gito had compassion and would have succoured the distressed Eumolpus. Upon which, my anger being still up, I gave the head of the merciful coxcomb two or three blows with my fist. He retired to the bed and fell a crying, but I so eagerly plied the hole I made my eyes relieve each other and, encouraging the mob to persist in assaulting Eumolpus, fed myself with the pleasing spectacle of his misfortunes, when the bailiff of the tenement, one Bargates, whom the scuffle had raised from supper, was brought into the room, supported by the legs of others, for he was so troubled by the gout he could not use his own. And having in his clownish manner with a great deal of heat made a long harangue against drunkards and vagabonds, looking on Eumolpus, "Ha! What! Is it you,"

says he, "most excellent of poets? What! These rogues
of slaves be not gone on the instant and dare raise their
hands against you!" «And without more ado, up he goes
to Eumolpus and whispering,» "I have a maid," says he,
"that flouts me when I ask her the question. Prithee, if
you have any love for me, lampoon her into better
manners."

While Eumolpus was thus privily engaged with Bar-
gates, the crier of the town, together with the constable
and a great concourse of people, entered the inn and,
shaking a torch that gave out more smoke than light,
mouths out to this effect, *viz.*:

NOT LONG AGO, RUN AWAY FROM THE BATH,
A BOY, ABOUT SIXTEEN YEARS OLD,
WITH CURLED HAIR AND NO MORALS,
VERY PRETTY, ANSWERS TO THE NAME GITO.
IF ANY MAN OR WOMAN, IN CITY OR COUNTRY,
CAN TELL TALE OR TIDINGS OF HIM,
SHALL HAVE FOR HIS REWARD
ONE THOUSAND SESTERCES.

Not far from the crier stood Ascyltos clad in a coat of
many colours, who, to encourage any discoverer, held
the reward in a silver charger before him. Upon this I
ordered Gito to steal under the bed and thrust his feet
and hands through the cords, that, as Ulysses formerly
hid himself under a bell-wether, so extended he might
cheat the searchers. Gito immediately obeyed the mo-
tion and, fixing himself as I directed, outdid Ulysses in

his native art. But that I might leave no room for suspicion I so disposed the bedclothes that none could believe any more than myself had lain there.

We had just done when Ascyltos with a beadle, having searched the other chambers, came to ours, which gave him greater hopes because he found the door close barred. But the constable he brought along with him with an iron crow forced it open. Upon Ascyltos's entry I threw myself at his feet and beseeched him if he had any memory for our past friendship or any respect for one that had shared misfortunes with him he would at least let me once more see Gito, who was still dear to me. And to give my sham entreaties a better colour, "I see," says I, "Ascyltos, you are come with designs on my life, for to what other end could you bring hither those ministers of justice? Therefore satisfy your rage, behold my naked bosom, let out that blood that under pretence of a search you come to seek!"

Ascyltos, now laying aside his old grudge, professed he came in pursuit of nothing but Gito, who had run away from him, and he did not desire the death of any man, much less of one who submitted to his mercy and for whom, notwithstanding the fatal quarrel, he had still a great kindness. The constable put me to more pains, for taking a stick out of the cook's hand, he felt under the bed with it and run it into every hole he found in the wall. Gito drew his body out of the stick's way and, breathing as gently as fear could make him, held his mouth close to the very bed bugs.

«They were hardly gone ere» Eumolpus bounced in upon us, for the broken door could stop nobody, and in a great heat cried out, "I'll earn the reward! I'll run after the crier and to give you due payment for your treachery I'll tell him that Gito is in your hands!" Eumolpus pursuing his design, I kissed his knees and entreated him not to hasten the end of dying men. "You would be justly angry," added I, "if you could discover the fugitive to them. The boy run into the crowd undiscovered and where he is gone I myself don't know. I beseech you, Eumolpus, bring me back the boy or even restore him to Ascyltos."

Just as I had worked him to a belief, Gito, with restraining his breath, sneezed thrice so loudly that he shook the bed. At which Eumolpus, turning about, saluted him with "God bless you, sir!" and, throwing off the bedclothes, saw the little Ulysses, who might have raised compassion even in a bloodthirsty Cyclops. Then looking upon me, "Thou villain," says he, "how have you bantered me? Durst you not tell truth even when you was catched in your roguery? If some god that has the care of human affairs had not forced the boy to discover himself I, poor fool, should be wandering round all the taverns." . . . But Gito, that could fawn much better than I, took a cobweb dipped in oil and applied it to the wound in his forehead, then, exchanging his mantle for the other's torn coat, embraced the half-reconciled Eumolpus and stuck to his lips; then at last he spoke. "Our lives," said he, "most indulgent father, our lives are in your power. If you love your Gito begin by preserving him. O! that I might perish by fire or water, I that am the cause of all these dissensions. My death would restore you to each other's friendship."

«Eumolpus, concerned at our grief, and particularly mindful of Gito's tenderness to him, "Surely," says he, "you are the greatest of fools who have souls enriched with virtues that can make you happy, yet live a continued martyrdom raising to yourselves every day new occasions of grief.» I, wherever I am, make my life as pleasant and free from trouble as if I expected no more of it. «Ascyltos haunts you here; avoid him by changing climates. I am taking a voyage to a foreign country and should be glad of your company. I believe to-morrow night I shall go on board the vessel. I am very well known there and you need not doubt of a civil entertainment."

His advice appeared to be both wise and profitable, for at once it delivered me from Ascyltos and gave me hopes of living more happily than I had done. Thus obliged by Eumolpus's good nature, I was sorry for the late injury I had done him and began to repent of my jealousy since it had occasioned so many disasters.»

At last with tears I beseeched him to be friends with me too, for that it was not in a rival's power to bound his rage, yet that I would try neither to say or do anything that might give just reason of offence, and hoped so wise and good a man as he would absolutely blot from his mind all marks of our former quarrels. For 'twas with men as with countries, on rude and neglected grounds snows lie very long, but where the fruitful earth was improved by culture they presently melt off and hardly leave a print behind. Thus, rough and unpolished minds can't discharge their passions suddenly, but where souls are enriched with instruction they but appear and vanish. "And to confirm the truth of what you say," returned Eumolpus, "all my heat expires in this kiss. But to prevent the designs of your enemies make ready your wallets and either follow me or, if you like it, act as leaders." He had not done speaking when, hearing the door move, we turned about and saw a seaman with a beard that made him appear terrible and grim, who saluted Eumolpus with a "Why d'ye stay, as if you did not know how near the time 'twas?" All immediately prepare for the journey. Eumolpus loads his servant, who had been all this time asleep; I and Gito packed up our things together and, thanking our stars, entered the vessel.

«We placed ourselves as much out of the way as we could under deck and, it being not yet day, Eumolpus fell asleep. I and Gito could not take a wink and I began to reflect.» " 'Tis pity the boy is so pleasing to my guest. But what of it? Is it so troublesome to share what we love when the best of nature's works are in common? The sun dispenses his rays on all. The moon with her infinite train of stars serves to light even beasts to their fodder. What below can boast an excellence of nature above the waters? Yet they flow in public for the use of all. Only love seems sweeter stolen than when it's given us. So it is, we esteem nothing unless 'tis envied by others. But what have I to fear in a rival that age and impotence conspire to render disagreeable, who when he has an inclination his body jades under him before he can reach his goal!" When I had cheated myself with this assurance I muffled my head in my coat and feigned myself asleep.

But on a sudden, as if fortune had resolved to ruin my quiet, I heard one above deck groaning out, "And has he scorned me?" This struck me with a trembling, for it was a man's voice and one I was afraid I knew. At a greater distance but with the same heat I heard a woman lamenting. "O that some god," said she, "would bring my Gito to my arms! How would I receive the prodigal!" So unexpected an accident turned us as pale as death. I especially, as though troubled by a nightmare, was a long time speechless. At last, trembling with fear, I pulled Eumolpus, who was now asleep, by the coat and, "I beseech you, father," said I, "who is the owner of this vessel and what passengers has he on board?" He was very angry to be disturbed. "And was it for this reason," said he, "that you chose the most private place in the ship, that none but yourself might disturb us? Or what will it signify if I tell you that one Lycas the Tarentine owns her and is carrying the lady Tryphaena back to Tarentum?"

For a while I stood like one thunderstruck, when opening my bosom I trembling cried out, "At last, For-

tune, thou hast entirely vanquished me!" For Gito, my better half, leaned on my breast and seemed to be rather dead than living. Our fear put us into a sweat and, after our sweating had a little recovered our spirits, I fell at the feet of Eumolpus and entreated him to have compassion of two dying wretches. "In the name of our mutual learning, lend us your hand. Our last hour has come and, unless you refuse us your help, it may even be welcome." Eumolpus was glad to serve us and swore by all that's sacred he was privy to no design against us and that he had very innocently brought us hither for no other end but our company, having hired his passage before he was acquainted with us. "But what practices are here against your lives?" added he, "or what Hannibal is our fellow passenger? Why, 'tis Lycas of Tarentum, a very honest man, that is both captain and owner of the vessel, and also master of a very plentiful estate in land, who, having an inclination to merchandize, freights his ship with his own cargo. Is this the terrible Cyclops? Is this the dreadful cut-throat we must pay our carriage to? And there is also Tryphaena, most beautiful of women, who travels hither and yon for her pleasure!" "These are the very two," replied Gito, "we strove to avoid," and in a low voice made Eumolpus, who trembled at the story, at once understand the cause of their malice and our present danger.

Eumolpus was so distracted in his thoughts he could not advise but bid us each give him his opinion. "And presume," says he, "we had just entered the Cyclops' den. We must seek a means of delivery, unless we design to free us from all danger by sinking the vessel." "No, no," began Gito, "rather offer the pilot a reward to steer the vessel to some port. And affirm the sea so disagrees with your friend that if he is not so kind you fear he'll die. You may colour the pretence with tears and appear so much concerned that, moved with compassion, the pilot may grant your request."

Eumolpus replied: "This is impossible to be effected because great ships with much difficulty are conducted into harbour. Besides it would seem unlikely that my friend should be so dangerously ill of a sudden. Add to this that Lycas may think himself obliged in civility to visit his sick passenger. Can you propose to escape by a means that will discover ye? But presuming the ship could be stopped when under full sail and that Lycas should omit visiting his sick on board, how can we get out but all must see? With our heads muffled or bare? If muffled, we move everyone to lend a hand to sick persons; if bare, what is it but to discover ourselves?"

"A desperate disease," said I, "must have a desperate cure. I know no better expedient of our delivery than to get into the long boat and by cutting the cord leave the rest to Fortune. Nor do I desire Eumolpus to share the danger, for what would it signify to involve an innocent person in other men's misfortunes? We shall think ourselves happy if Fortune be kind."

" 'Twas not ill advised," said Eumolpus, "if it could be done; for do you think to stir in the ship unobserved when the distant motion of the stars themselves can't escape the pilot's vigilance? Were he to nod, you might make your escape from another part of the ship, but you must let yourselves down by the stern, by the very rudder, where the hawser of the boat is fastened. Besides, Encolpius, I wonder you did not remember that in the boat itself there is constantly a sailor on duty, nor will he be moved from his post without you cut his throat or fling him overboard, which consider whether you can dare attempt. For my part, to go with you I would refuse no danger where there was the least hopes of getting off, but to put so low a value on life, to throw it away as a useless thing, I believe even yourselves are unwilling. Hear whether you like my proposal. I'll put you into two trunks I have here and, making holes for you to breathe and eat through, will place you amongst my other baggage. To-morrow morning I'll alarm the whole ship, crying out my servants, fearing a greater punishment in the night, jumped into the sea, that when the ship makes to land I may carry you off in my baggage."

"Very well," said I, "but will you inclose us so that nature will not be troublesome with her evacuations, and can you insure us from snoring if asleep or sneezing if awake, or, because I once succeeded in a like deceit, must we meet a second time with the same success? But suppose we could hold out a day so tied up, what shall we do if we are delayed by a calm or a storm? Clothes long bound up rot at the pleats and folded parchments lose their shape. Can we, do you think, that are young and not inured to labour, endure to be packed and bound up like statues? . . . Since we are yet to seek a way of escape, for no proposal has been made without an objection, see what I have thought on. The studious Eumolpus, I presume, never goes without ink. Is there a better expedient than washing our hands, face, and hair with that, to appear like Ethiopian slaves, when, without putting ourselves on the rack, we can't but be merry to act a cheat that so neatly imposes on our enemies?"

"And why would you not have us circumcised too," interrupted Gito, "that we may appear like Jews, and have our ears bored to persuade them we came from Arabia? And why did you not advise our faces to be chalked that we might pass for Frenchmen? As if our colour alone would make such a mighty alteration, and many other signs would not have to agree to carry off so great a lie! Grant our daubed faces would keep their colour, suppose it would not wash off, nor our clothes stick to the ink, which often happens even when glue is not added, how can we imitate their swollen lips? the short curl of their hair? the marks on their foreheads? their circular way of walking? their splay feet or the mode of their beards? An artificial colour rather stains than alters the body. But if you'll be ruled by a madman let's cover our heads and jump into the sea."

"Nor God nor man," cried Eumolpus, "could suffer you make so ill an end; rather pursue this advice: My servant, as you may imagine by his razor, is a piece of a barber. Let him not only shave your heads but, as a mark of greater punishment, your eyebrows too, and I'll finish your disguise with an inscription on your foreheads, that you may appear as slaves branded for some extraordinary villainy. Thus the same letters will at once divert suspicion and conceal your countenances under the mask of punishment."

We liked the advice and hastened to the execution, when, stealing to the side of the vessel, we committed our heads and eyebrows to the barber. Eumolpus, in the meantime, filled our forehead with great letters, and very liberally dispensed the known marks of fugitives through the other parts of our faces. One of the passengers, easing his stomach over the side of the ship and by the moon perceiving a barber busy at so unseasonable a time, cursing the omen that he thought presaged a shipwreck, ran to his hammock. We, though pretending little care for his curses, were much concerned and, the noise over, spent the rest of the night without resting much.

«The next day Eumolpus, when he found Tryphaena was stirring, went to visit Lycas and after he had talked with him about the happy voyage he hoped from the clearness of the heavens, Lycas, turning to Tryphaena,» "Methoughts about midnight the vision of Priapus appeared to me and told me he had lately brought into my ship Encolpius whom I sought for." Tryphaena was startled and, "You'd swear we had slept together," re-

plied she, "for methoughts the image of Neptune that I saw in the cloisters at Baiae told me that in Lycas's ship I should meet my Gito." "Hence proceeds," said Eumolpus, interrupting 'em, "that veneration I pay the divine Epicurus, who with so much wit has discovered such illusions!—

When in a dream presented to our view
Those airy forms appear so like the true,
Nor heaven nor hell the fancied visions sends
But every breast its own delusion lends.
For when soft sleep the body wraps in ease
And from the heavy mass our fancy frees,
Whatever 'tis in which we take delight
And think of most by day, we dream at night.
Th' ambitious brave who mighty states o'erturn,
Ruin whole empires and vast cities burn,

From fancied darts believe a darkened sky
And see in haste retreating squadrons fly.
Here conscious plains a bloody prospect yield
And all the purple horrors of the field;
There kings deceased with wondrous pomp of woe
Late to the grave in sad procession go.
He that by day litigious knots untied
And charmed the drowsy bench to either side,
By night a crowd of cringing clients sees,
Smiles on the fools and kindly takes their fees.
The miser views his glittering heaps of gold
And oft the visionary sums are told,
Then fancies thieves disturb his short delight
He views their masks and wakens with the fright.
To heaven the merchant does himself address,
Dreaming of wrecks, religious in distress.
Huntsmen with joy the imagined chase pursue,
Halloo aloud and see the stag in view.
The mistress to her distant lover writes
And, as awake, with flames and darts indites.
The good wife dreaming of her stallion's charms
Oft seeks the pleasure in her cuckold's arms.
Dogs in full cry in sleep the hare pursue
And hapless wretches their old griefs renew."

But when Lycas had by prayer averted the ill-omen of
Tryphaena's dream, "That we may not seem," said he,
"to slight the divine powers, what hinders but we search
the vessel?" Upon which, one Aesius, the passenger that
had discovered us so unseasonably, cried out: "These are
the men that were shaved by moonshine to-night. Heav-
en avert the omen! I thought the ceremony of cutting

the nails and hair was never performed but as a solemn sacrifice to appease a storm."

"Is't so?" says Lycas in a great heat. "Did any in the ship offer to shave themselves and at midnight too? Bring 'em quickly hither that I may know who they are that deserve to die a sacrifice for our safety." " 'Twas I," said Eumolpus, "commanded it, not wishing ill to the ship in which I travel but ease to myself. For being wicked slaves and having long staring hairs, I ordered the uncomely sight to be taken away, not only that I might not seem to make a prison of the ship, but that the mark of their villainy might more plainly appear, and to let you know how richly they deserve the punishment. Among other rogueries, they robbed me of a considerable sum of money and spent it in luxury and debauches on a trull that was at both their services, whom I catched them with last night. In short, they yet smell of the wine they profusely gave themselves with my money."

Lycas, that the offenders might atone for their crime, ordered each of 'em forty stripes. We were immediately brought to the place of execution where the enraged seamen set upon us with ropes-ends and tried to offer our blood a sacrifice for their safety. I bore three stripes very heroically. Gito, who had not so much passive valour, at the first blow set up such an outcry that the well known sound of his voice reached Tryphaena's ear who, in great disorder, attended with her maids that were equally surprised, ran to the sufferer.

Gito's admirable beauty had already softened even the sailors' rage and seemed without speaking to entreat their favour when the maids unanimously cried out: " 'Tis Gito! 'Tis Gito! Hold your barbarous hands! Help, madam, 'tis Gito!" Tryphaena hastened to their outcries, already convinced from whence those complaints proceeded, and with eager haste flew to the boy.

Upon which Lycas, that knew me very well, as if he had heard my voice, ran to me and, without considering my face or hands, directed his gaze on my genitals, towards which he stretched an officious hand and, "Your servant, Encolpius!" says he. 'Tis no wonder that the nurse of Ulysses discovered him after twenty years' absence by a scar on his forehead, when the most prudent Lycas, though all body and face was disguised, discovered his fugitive by the one remaining sign.

Tryphaena, having cheated herself into a belief that those marks of slavery we wore on our foreheads were real, wept, and began in a low voice to enquire what prison had stopped us in our rambles or whose cruel hands could inflict such a punishment without reluctance. Though fugitives who had repaid her goodness with hatred doubtless deserved some punishment.

Lycas was in great heat at Tryphaena's tenderness. And, "Thou foolish woman," said he, "can you believe that these wounds were produced by an iron that formed these letters! Would they had been so branded in reality; that had afforded us the greatest consolation. Now we are mocked by the tricks of the play-house and bantered with a false inscription." Tryphaena, not yet unmindful of our former amours, would have pitied us, when Lycas, still resenting the abuse he received in his vitiated wife and the affronts at the porch of Hercules's temple, with greater rage cried out: "I thought, Tryphaena, you had been convinced that heaven has the care of human affairs, when it not only brought our imprudent enemies into our power but revealed what it had done in a vision to us both. See what you'll get by pardoning them, whom heaven itself has brought to punishment. For my part I am not naturally so cruel, but am afraid the judgement I should prevent from justly falling upon others may light on my own head." This superstitious harangue turned Tryphaena from hindering our punishment to hasten its execution, for she had suffered as great affronts as Lycas when her honour and chastity were slighted at a public meeting.

«When Lycas found Tryphaena was as eagerly inclined to revenge as himself, he ordered our punishments to be increased which, when Eumolpus perceived, he endeavoured to mitigate his passion after this manner. "I pity the wretches," said he, "that lie at your mercy. Lycas, they implore your compassion.» They have chosen me as a man, I believe, not unknown to fame, for their advocate to reconcile them to their former dearest friends. Can you believe 'twas by accident they fell into your hands when all passengers make it their chief business to enquire to whose care they are to trust themselves. When you are satisfied of their intentions can you be so barbarous to continue your revenge? Suffer, therefore, free-born men to pursue their intended voyage without injury. Even cruel and implacable masters allay their cruelty when their slaves repent, and all give quarter to the enemy that surrenders himself. What can you or will you desire more? You have at your feet repenting supplicants; they're gentlemen and men of worth, and, what's more prevailing than both, were once caressed as your dearest friends. Had they robbed you of your money or betrayed your trust, by Hercules! the punishment they've inflicted on themselves might have satisfied your rage. Don't you see on their faces the marks of slaves who, though free, to atone their injuries to you have branded themselves in so slavish a manner?"

"Do not confound the matter," interrupted Lycas, "but take it in order. And first of all, if they came with design to surrender themselves, why did they cut off their hair? For all disguises are assumed rather to deceive than satisfy the injured. Next, if they expected to ingratiate themselves by their ambassador, why have you endeavoured in everything to conceal them you were to speak for? Whence it plainly appears 'twas by accident the offenders fell into the trap and that you have used this artifice to help them escape their deserved punishment. Sure you thought to prejudice the spectators against us by ringing in our ears that they were gentlemen and men of worth, but have a care their cause don't suffer by your assurance. What should the

injured do when the guilty come to them to be pun-
ished? And if they were our friends they deserve to be
more severely treated, for he that wrongs a stranger is
called a rogue, but he that serves a friend so, is little less
than a parricide."

"I am sensible," said Eumolpus, answering this dread-
ful harangue, "that nothing could happen to these un-
happy men more unfortunate than the cutting their hair
off at midnight, which is the only argument that may
persuade you to mistake their voluntary coming here
for accidental. But I shall as candidly endeavour to un-
deceive you as it was innocently acted. Before they em-
barked they designed to ease their heads of that as a
troublesome and useless weight, but the unexpected
wind that hastened us on board made them defer it. Nor
did they suspect it to be of any moment when and where
'twas done, being equally ignorant of the ill omens and
customs of mariners."

"What advantage," replied Lycas, "could they pro-
pose to themselves by being thus shorn? Unless they
thought baldness might sooner raise our compassion.
And what need has truth of an advocate?" When, ad-
dressing himself to me, "What sayest thou, bandit?"
said he. "What rat has gnawed off your eyebrows? To
what god have you offered your hair? Answer, poi-
soner!"

The fear of punishment struck me speechless, nor
could I find anything to urge in my defence against so
plain an accusation. The confusion I was in, my dis-

figured face, and the baldness of my head and eyebrows gave a ridiculous air to everything I said or did. But when they wiped us with a wet sponge, the letters, melting into one, spread over our faces such a sooty cloud that it turned Lycas's rage into perfect loathing. Eumolpus could not endure to see free-born men, against all law and justice, so abused and, returning their savage threats with blows, not only was our advocate but champion too. He was seconded by his man and two or three sick passengers appeared our friends, that served rather to encourage us than increase our force.

Upon which I was so far from begging pardon that without any respect I shook my fists at Tryphaena and plainly told her she should feel me if her lecherous lady-ship, who alone in the ship deserved a flogging, was not content to decline her pretensions to Gito. The angry Lycas was all in a rage at my impudence and very impatient for revenge when he found, without being concerned for my own cause, I only stood up for another's. Nor was Tryphaena less disturbed at my contempt of her, at what time every one in the vessel chose his side and put himself in a posture of defence.

On our side, Eumolpus's servant distributed to us the instruments of his trade and reserved a razor for his own defence. On the other, Tryphaena and her attendants advanced armed with nothing but their nails and tongues, which last supplied the want of drums in the army. The pilot alone, crying out, threatened he would leave the ship to the mercy of the waves if they continued the bustle raised about the lust of two or three vagabonds. This did not in the least retard the fight; they pressing for revenge, we for our lives. In short many fell half dead on both sides; others withdrew, as from great armies, to be dressed of their wounds, yet this damps not the rage of either side.

Then the bold Gito, drawing out that part of him Tryphaena most admired, clapped a bloody razor to it and threatened to cut away the cause of all our misfortune. But Tryphaena flew to prevent so great a crime and clearly revealed her forgiveness. I often offered at my throat too, but with as little design to kill myself as Gito to do what he threatened. He the more boldly handled his weapon because he knew it to be the same blunt razor he had used before. Upon this, both sides again drew up their ranks and the fight was about to be renewed on different terms when the pilot with much ado persuaded Tryphaena to be the herald of a truce.

Articles according to the custom of countries being immediately struck up on both sides, she snatched an olive branch from the image of the ship's guardian deity and, holding it in the midst of us, thus addressed herself:

> Great Gods! What fury does your mind enrage?
> What sudden madness arms you to engage?
> Not here her brother curst Medea slays,
> Nor Paris here a guilty flame obeys
> And lovely ruin to his Troy conveys.
> But slighted vows these dire misfortunes send,
> And the wronged god does for his fame contend.
> The Ocean swells, and the tempestuous wind
> Is, like our humours, fierce and unconfined.
> Without, the waves a threatening war begin
> And love has raised a dreadful storm within.
> Exposed to nature's quarrels and our own,
> For former feuds by gentle peace atone.
> Nor let your wild ungoverned passions be
> Rough as the wind or angry as the sea.

When in a great heat Tryphaena had thus expressed herself, both armies stood still a while and, reviving the treaty of peace, put a stop to the war. Our captain, Eumolpus, prudently used the occasion of her repentance and, having first severely reprimanded Lycas, signed the articles which were as follow:

"Tryphaena, you do from the bottom of your heart, as you are in perfect mind, promise never to complain of any injury you have received from Gito; nor mention, upbraid him with, or study to revenge, directly or indirectly, any action of his before this day; and to prevent your forcing him to an unwilling compliance be it further agreed that you never kiss, coll, or bring him to a closer hug without his consent, upon the pain and forfeiture of one hundred denarii, to be counted out before witnesses.

"Item: You, Lycas, from the bottom of your heart, as you are in perfect mind, do promise never to reproach or insultingly treat Encolpius either in words or gestures, and never to enquire where he sleeps o' nights; and for every time you should do so you will forfeit two hundred denarii."

Conditions thus agreed on, we laid down our arms, and lest any grudge might still remain we wiped off the memory of all things past in repeated kisses. All parties desiring peace, our quarrels vanished, and a sumptuous banquet on the very field of battle spread an air of mirth through the whole company. And now, a sudden calm hindering the ship from making any way, the crew betook themselves to several diversions. Here an angler bobbed for fish that, rising, seemed with haste to meet their ruin; there another draws the unwilling prey that he had betrayed with an inviting bait. When looking up, we saw sea-birds sitting on the sail yards about which one skilled in the art of fowling had placed lime twigs and made them his booty. Their down feathers flew about the air or swam on the slow surges of the sea.

Now Lycas began again to be friends with me, and Tryphaena, as a mark of her love, poured the dregs of her wine over Gito. At what time Eumolpus, quite

drunk, aimed at raillery on those that were bald and
branded, till, having spent his stock of jests, he returned
to his verses and, designing an elegy on the loss of our
hair, thus began:

> Nature's chief ornament, the hair, is lost;
> Those blooming locks feel an autumnal frost.
> Now the bald temples mourn their banished shade
> And blushes spread over the sunburnt head.
> The charms deceitful nature first does pay
> Our youth, alas, it snatches first away.

> Unhappy mortal! that but now
> The lovely grace of hair did'st know,
> Bright as the sun or Cynthia's beams,
> Now worse than brass, and only seems
> A mushroom that in garden teems.
> From sporting girls you'll frighted run
> And know that death you cannot shun,
> Now that your head's best part is done.

He would have condemned us to hear more and I be-
lieve worse than the former if an attendant of Try-
phaena had not taken Gito below deck and dressed him
up in her mistress's peruque. And to restore him per-
fectly to his former figure she took a pair of false eye-
brows out of her ladies' patch-box and set them on so
exactly, nature might have mistaken them for her own
work. At the sight of the true Gito, Tryphaena wept for
joy, who could not before embrace him with so real a
satisfaction. I was glad to see his loss so well repaired,
yet often hid my head as sensible I appeared more than

commonly deformed, when even Lycas thought me not worth speaking to. But 'twas not long ere the same maid came to my relief and, calling me aside, dressed me in a wig no less agreeable, for being of a golden colour it rather improved my complexion.

But Eumolpus, our advocate and reconciler, to entertain the company and keep up the mirth, began to be pleasant on the inconstancy of women: how forward they were to love and how soon they forgot their sparks. And no woman was so chaste but her untried lust might be raised to a fury. Nor would he bring instances from ancient tragedies or personages notorious in antiquity, but was ready to entertain us, if we would please to hear, with a story within the circle of his own memory. Upon which the eyes and ears of all were devoted to him and he thus began:

"There was at Ephesus a lady of so celebrated a reputation that the women of even neighbouring nations came to pay their respects to her as a person of extraordinary virtue. This lady, at the death of her husband, not content with tearing her hair or beating her breasts, those common expressions of grief, followed him into the vault—where, after the Grecian custom, the body had been placed in a monument—to watch the corpse, and whole days and nights continued weeping. The persuasions of parents and relations could neither divert her grief or make her take anything to preserve life. At last even the magistrates had to retire, and thus, lamented by all for so singular an example of grief, she lived five days without eating.

"All left her but a faithful maid whose tears flowed as fast as her afflicted lady's, and who, when the lamp they had by them began to flicker, renewed the light. By this time she became the talk of the whole town and all degrees of men confessed she was the only true example of love and chastity.

"In the meantime the governor of the province ordered some outlaws to be crucified near the vault in which the lady was weeping over the corpse of her late husband. The soldier that guarded the bodies, lest any might be taken from the cross and buried, upon his watch observed a light in the vault and, hearing the groans of some afflicted person, pressed with the curiosity common to all mankind, he desired to know who or what it was. Upon which he entered the vault and, seeing a very beautiful woman, amazed at first, he fancied it was a spirit; but viewing the dead body and considering her tears and torn face he soon guessed the truth, that the lady could not bear the loss of her husband. He brings his supper with him into the vault and began to persuade the mournful lady not to continue her unnecessary grief nor with vain complaints consume her health; that death was common to all men and the grave the universal abode, and such other commonplaces as are used to restore afflicted persons to calmness. But she, moved anew by the comfort a stranger offered, redoubled her grief and, tearing her hair, cast it on the body that lay before her.

"The soldier, however, did not withdraw, but with the like invitations offered her somewhat to eat, till the maid, overcome, I presume, by the pleasing scent of the wine, no longer could resist the soldier's courtesy. When refreshed with the entertainment she began to join her persuasions to win her lady. 'And what advantage,' said she, 'would you reap in starving yourself to death, in burying yourself alive? What would it signify to anticipate your fate? Do buried ghosts and ashes feel our care? Do you wish, Madam, to come to life again? Will you shake off these vain complaints, the marks of our sex's weakness, and enjoy the world while you may? The very body that lies there should advise you to make the best of life.'

"No one listens with reluctance when commanded to eat or live. The lady, now dry with so long fasting, suffered herself to be overcome, nor was she less pleased with her entertainment than her maid who first surrendered. You know with what thoughts encouraging

meats inspire young persons. With the same charms our
soldier had won her to be in love with life he addressed
himself to her as a lover, nor did his person appear less
agreeable to the chaste lady than his conversation. And
the maid, to raise her opinion of him, quoted Virgil:
'And will you fight e'en against pleasing love?'

"To make short, nor even in this could the lady deny
him anything, and thus our victorious soldier succeeded
in both. She received his embraces not only that night
they struck up the bargain, but the next, and the night
after that, having shut the door of the vault, that if any
of her acquaintance or strangers had come out of curios-
ity to see her they might have believed the most chaste
of all women had expired by the body of her husband.
Our soldier was so taken with his beautiful mistress and
the privacy of enjoying her that the little money he was
master of he laid out for her entertainment and, as soon
as 'twas night, conveyed it into the vault.

"In the meantime, the relations of one of the malefac-
tors, finding the body unguarded, took it from the cross
and buried it. The soldier, thus robbed while he was in
the vault, the next day, when he perceived one of the
bodies gone, dreading the usual punishment, told the
lady what had happened and added that with his own
sword he would prevent the judge's sentence if she but
please give him burial and make that place at once the
fatal monument of a lover and a husband. The lady, not
less merciful than chaste, cried out: 'May the Gods
never allow me to feel the loss of the only two men in

the world I hold most dear. I'd rather hang up the dead body of the one than be the wicked instrument of the other's death!' Upon which she ordered her husband's body to be taken out of the coffin and fixed to the cross in the room of that which was wanting. Our soldier pursued the directions of the discreet lady and the next day the people wondered by what means a dead man had been able to get himself on to a cross."

The seamen laughed at the story, while Tryphaena, not a little ashamed, applied her cheek to Gito's and hid her blushes. But Lycas wore an air of displeasure and, knitting his brows, "If the governor," said he, "had been a just man, he ought to have restored the husband's body to his monument and hung the woman on the cross." I don't doubt it made him reflect on his own wife and the whole scene of our lust when we robbed the vessel. But the articles of our treaty obliged him not to complain and the mirth that engaged us gave him no opportunity to vent his rage. Tryphaena entertained herself in Gito's arms, pressing oft his neck with eager kisses and oft disposing his new ornaments to make them appear more agreeable to his face.

At this I was not a little out of humour and, impatient of our new league, could neither eat nor drink anything, but with side looks wished a thousand curses on them both. Every kiss and every look she gave him wounded me. Nor did I yet know whether I had more reason to reproach the boy for seducing my mistress or my mistress for corrupting the boy. Both were displeasing

to my eyes and sadder by far than my former captivity.
And to complete my misery neither Tryphaena spoke
to me as if I had been her acquaintance and once be-
loved, nor did Gito think me worth drinking to or,
what's the least he could do, attempt to bring me into
the common discourse. I believe he was tender of the
new return of her favours and afraid to give her another
occasion to fall out with him. Grief forced a flood of
tears from my eyes and I stifled my complaints till I was
ready to expire.

«When Lycas perceived how well, though in this
trouble, my yellow ornament became me, he was in-
flamed afresh and,» viewing me with lover's eyes, ad-
dressed himself as such, when, laying aside the haughty
brow of a master, he put on the tender complacency of
a friend. But his endeavours were fruitless. «At last,
meeting with an entire repulse, his love turning to fury,
he endeavoured to ravish the favours he could not win
by entreaty, at what time Tryphaena came in and ob-
serving his wantonness, in the greatest confusion he hid
his head and ran from her.

Upon which the more lustful Tryphaena asked and
made me tell her what those wanton caresses meant.
She was inspired with new heat at the relation and,
mindful of our old amours, offered to revive our former
commerce but, worn off my legs with these employ-
ments, I gave her invitations but an ill return. Yet she,
with all the desires of a woman transported by her pas-
sion, threw her arms about me and so closely locked me

in her embraces I was forced to cry out. One of her
maids came in at the noise and, easily believing I would
force from her the favours I had denied her mistress,
rushed between and loosed the bands. Tryphaena, meet-
ing with such a repulse and even raging with desire,
took it more grievous at my hands and, with threats at
her going off, flew to Lycas, not only to raise his resent-
ment against me but to join with him in pursuit of
revenge.

By the way, observe I had formerly been well re-
ceived by this attendant of Tryphaena when I main-
tained a commerce with her mistress. Upon that score
she resented my converse with Tryphaena and, deeply
sighing, made me eager to know the occasion. When
she, stepping back, thus began:» "If you had any sparks
of a gentleman in you, you'd value her no more than a
common prostitute. If you were a man you would not
descend to such a jakes." «These thoughts not a little
disturbed her, but» I was ashamed of nothing more than
that Eumolpus, suspecting the occasion, should in his
next verses make our supposed quarrel the subject of his
drollery «and lest my care to avoid it should prove one
means of discovering it.

When I was contriving how to prevent his suspicion,
Eumolpus himself came in, already acquainted with
what was done. For Tryphaena had communicated her
grief to Gito and endeavoured, at his cost, to compen-
sate the injury I had offered her. On which, Eumolpus
was on fire, and the more because her wantonness was

an open breach of the articles she had signed. When the old doctor saw me, pitying my misfortune, he desired to know the whole scene from myself. I freely told him of the gamesomeness of Lycas, and Tryphaena's lustful assault, that he was already well informed of. Upon which,» in a solemn oath, he swore «to vindicate our cause and that heaven was too just to suffer so many crimes to go unpunished.»

While we were thus engaged a storm arose. Now thick clouds and the enraged flood eclipsed the day. The seamen fly to their posts as fast as fear could make them, and pulling down the sails let the ship ride the storm. For the wind, often veering, made them hopeless of any direct course, nor did the pilot know which way to steer. Sometimes the ungovernable ship was forced on the coast of Sicily; often the North wind seized it and tossed it near the shores of Italy; and what was more dangerous than all, on a sudden, the gathering clouds spread such a horrid darkness all around that the pilot could not see even the fore-castle. Upon which, all despairing for safety, Lycas threw himself before me and lifting up his trembling hands, "I beseech you, Encolpius," began he, "assist the distressed! Restore to the ship the sacred vest and timbrel of Isis! Be merciful, as is your custom!" At what time a whirlwind snatched him up and threw him howling amidst the flood and soon a spiteful wave just showed him us and drew him back again. Tryphaena would have suffered the same fate but she was hastily taken up by her faithful servants and placed with her

chief goods in the skiff and so avoided a most certain
death.

I, locked in Gito's arms, not without tears, cried out:
"And this we have merited of heaven, that only death
should join us! But even now I feel that fortune will be
against it. For see! The waves threaten to overset the
vessel, and now the tempest comes to burst the loved
bands that unite us! Therefore, if you really love En-
colpius, let's kiss while we may and snatch this last joy
even in spite of our approaching fate!" When I had thus
said, Gito threw off his mantle and, getting under mine,
thrust his head out at top to reach my lips, but that the
most malignant waves might not wash us asunder he
girt himself to me with his girdle and, " 'Tis some com-
fort," said he, "to think that by these means the sea will
bear us longer ere it can divorce us from each other's
arms. Or if in compassion it should throw us on the
same shore, either the next passer-by would give us a
monument of stones that by the common laws of hu-
manity he would cast upon us, or at least the angry
waves that seem to conspire against us would unwit-
tingly bury us in one grave with the sand their rage
would vomit up." I was satisfied with my bonds and,
as on my death-bed, did now contentedly expect the
coming hour.

In the meantime the tempest, acting the decrees of
fate, had rent all the rigging from the vessel: no mast,
no rudder left, not a rope or plank but an awkward
shapeless body of a ship tossed up and down the flood.

. . . The fishermen that inhabited the sea-side, expecting a booty, in all haste put out with their boats, but when they saw those in the vessel that could defend their own they changed their design of pillaging to succouring.

«After a salute on both sides,» unwonted murmurs, like that of some beast labouring to get out, proceeded from beneath the master's cabin. Upon which, following the sound, we found Eumolpus sitting alone and in his hand a large scroll of parchment that he was filling even to the margin with verses. We all were amazed to see a man amuse himself with poetry at a time when he had reason to think each minute would be his last, and having drawn him making a great noise, from his hole, we endeavoured to recover him from his frenzy, but he was in such a heat to be disturbed that " 'Sdeath," said he, "let me make an end to this couplet, the poem labours at the close." On which I took hold of the madman and ordered the still murmuring poet to be hauled on shore. When with some trouble we had got him there, we very pensively entered one of the fishermen's huts and, having supped as best we could on the provisions the salt water had spoiled, we passed the night in a very melancholy condition.

The next day as we were proposing how to bestow ourselves, I suddenly discovered a human body floating on a little wave that made to shore. I stood still, concerned, and began with tears in my eyes to look on the treacherous waters. "And who knows," I cried out, "but this wretch's wife, in some part of the world secure at home, may expect his coming, or a son ignorant of the fatal storm, or a father to whom he gave a parting kiss. These are our great designs! Vain mortals swell with promising hopes, yet there's the issue of them all!

See the mighty nothing, how it's tossed!" When I had thus bemoaned the wretch as one unknown, the sea cast him on land with his face, not much disfigured, toward heaven, upon which I made up to it and easily knew that the but now terrible and implacable Lycas was lying at my feet.

I could not restrain my tears but, beating my breast, "Now where's," said I, "your rage? where your unruly passions? Now you're exposed a prey for fish and beasts, and the poor shipwrecked wretch with all his boasted power now has not one plank of the great ship he proudly called his own. After this, let mortals flatter themselves with golden dreams and warily plan how to entail their ill-got wealth for a thousand years! 'Twas but yesterday this lifeless thing was poring over his ledgers and had fixed the very day he thought to return. How short, good God, is the poor wretch of his design! But 'tis not the sea alone we should fear. One the wars hurry to his death; another while at his devotions is buried under the ruins of his house; a third falling from his carriage hastens to his death; eating often kills the greedy, and abstinence, the temperate. If we rightly consider it, in this sea of life we may be shipwrecked everywhere. We vainly lament the want of burial to a wretch that's drowned, as if it concerned the perishing carcass whether flames, worms, or fishes were its cannibals. Whatever way you are consumed, the end of all's the same. Wild beasts will tear their bodies, as if teeth were less gentle than the flames. 'Tis indeed the punishment we believe is the highest we can inflict on slaves that have provoked us. Therefore what madness is it to trouble our lives with the cares of our burial after we are dead?"

After these reflections, we performed the last offices for the dead and, though his enemies, we honoured him with a funeral pile, but while Eumolpus was making an epitaph his eyes roamed here and there to find an image that might raise his fancy.

Having freely acquitted ourselves of this piece of humanity to Lycas we pursued our designed journey and, all in a sweat, soon reached the head of a neighbouring hill from whence we discovered a town seated on the top of a very high mountain. We did not know it till a shepherd informed us 'twas Crotona, the most ancient and once most flourishing city of Italy.

When we enquired of him what sort of people inhabited this renowned place and what kind of commerce they chiefly maintained, since they were impoverished by so many wars, "Gentlemen," said he, "if you have designs of trading you must go another way or change your plan of life. But if you're of the admired sort of men that have the thriving qualifications of lying and cheating you're in the direct path to business. For in this city no learning flourisheth, eloquence finds no room here, temperance, good manners nor any virtue can meet with a reward. Assure yourselves of finding here but two sorts of men, and they are the cheated and those that cheat. No one begets children, for he that has natural heirs dares not appear at any public game or show, is denied all public privileges and only herds among those that all men piss upon. But single men, who have no ties of nature that oblige the disposal of their wealth, are caressed by all and have the greatest honours conferred on them; they are the only valorous, the only brave, nay, and only innocent too. You're going to a city," added he, "like a field in plague time, in which there is nothing but carcasses being devoured and crows that devour them."

The prudent Eumolpus, at a thing so surprisingly new, began to be thoughtful and confessed that way to riches did not displease him. I believed it the effect of a poetic gaiety that had not left his years. When, "I wish," continued he, "I could maintain a greater figure as well in habit as attendance; 'twould give a better colour to my pretences. By Hercules, I would straightway take on the business and soon advance all our fortunes." Promising therefore to supply his wants, "We have with us," said I, "the sacred robe of Isis and all the booty we made at Lycurgus's villa; and as for cash, I am sure the great mother of the Gods with her accustomed grace will supply it for our current needs." "Why then," said Eumolpus, "do we delay casting our comedy? And if you like the proposal, let me be called your master."

None ever condemned a project that was no charge to him; therefore, to be true to his interests we engaged in a solemn oath, before we would discover the cheat, to suffer ten thousand racks. Thus, like free-born gladiators selling their liberty, we religiously devoted both our souls and bodies to our new master. After the solemn ceremonies of our oath were ended, like slaves at a distance we salute the master of our own making. He then instructed us on our parts, that our lord Eumolpus, grieved at the loss of a son who was a great orator and comfort to his age, was unhappily forced to quit the place of his abode lest the daily salutes of those that expected preferments under him, or the visits of his companions, or the sight of the monument, might be the continual occasions of tears. The late shipwreck had added to his grief, having lost to the value of twenty millions, though he was not so much concerned at the loss of his money as of his large retinue, the lack of which might impair the greatness of his dignity and honour. We were to add that our lord had thirty millions in Africa in estates and mortgages and so great a number of slaves dispersed about the farms in Numidia that he could raise a force able to sack Carthage.

After this, that his actions might agree with his condition, 'twas concluded necessary for him to wear an air of discontent; that he should with a stately stiffness, like quality, often cough and spit about the room; that he should complain of his stomach and condemn all dishes and ever talk of gold and silver, of estates that disappointed his expectations and of repeated bad harvests; moreover, that he should every day sit over his accounts and every month change his will. And that nothing might be wanting to complete the humour, as often as he had occasion to call any of us he should use one name for another, that it might easily appear how mindful our lord was even of the servants he had left in Africa.

Matters thus ordered, having, as all that would thrive, implored the blessing of heaven, we began our march. But both Gito did not like this new slavery, and Corax, Eumolpus's hired servant bearing most of our baggage, in a little time beginning to be uneasy in his service, would often rest his burden, and with ten thousand wry looks and as many curses for our going so fast at last swore he would either leave his charge or run away with it. " 'Sdeath," said he, "d'ye think I'm a pack-horse or a barge to be loaded with building stone? I was hired for a man, not a horse. Nor am I less of a gentleman by birth than any of you all, though my father left me in a mean condition." Not content with reproaches, but, getting before us, he lift up one leg and, venting his choler at the wrong end, filled our nostrils with a beastly scent. «Gito mocked his humour and for every crack he gave returned the like that one scent might stifle the other.

But even here Eumolpus, returning to his old humour, began:» "This poetry deceives many young men. For not only everyone that is able to give a verse its numbers and spin out his feeble sense in a long train of words has the vanity to think himself inspired, but pleaders at the bar when they would give themselves a-loose from business apply themselves to poetry, as an entertainment without trouble, believing it easier to compile a poem than maintain a controversy adorned with a few florid sentences. But neither will a generous spirit affect the empty sound of words nor can a mind, unless enriched with learning, be delivered of a birth of poetry. There must be purity of language; no porterly expression or meanness, as I may call it, of words is to be admitted, but a style perfectly above the common and with Horace

> Scorn the illiterate herd
> And drive them from you.

"Besides, you must be strictly diligent that your conceits may appear of a piece with the body of your discourse and your colours so laid that each may contribute to the beauty of the whole. Greece has given us Homer and the lyric poets for example; Rome, Virgil, and the painstaking niceness of Horace. Others either never saw the path that leads to poetry or, seeing, were afraid to tread it. To describe the civil wars of Rome would be a masterpiece; the unlettered head that offers at it will sink beneath the weight of so great a work. For to relate past actions is not so much the business of a poet as an historian. The boundless genius of a poet strikes through all mazes, introduces gods, and puts the invention on the rack for poetic ornaments, that it may rather seem a prophetic fury than a strict relation, with witnesses, of mere truth. As for example, this rapture, though I have not given it the last hand:

Now Rome reigned Empress o'er the vanquished ball,
As far as earth and seas, obeyed by all.
Uneasy, yet with more desires she's curst,
And boundless as her empire is her thirst.
In burdened vessels now they travelled o'er
The furrowed deep to seas unknown before,
And any hidden part of land or sea
That gold afforded was an enemy.
Thus fate the seeds of civil fury raised
When great in wealth no common pleasure pleased.
Rome scorns the dye which Tyrian altars boast
And seeks a nobler on the Iberian coast.
The purple of the sea contemned is grown;
India with silks, Africk with precious stone,
Arabia with her spices, hither come
And with their ruin raise the pride of Rome.
But other spoils, destructive to her peace,
Rome's ruin bode and future ills increase.
Through Libyan deserts are wild monsters chased
And the remotest parts of Africk traced,
Where the unwieldy elephant that's ta'en
For fatal value of his tooth is slain.
Now mottled tigers, eager to engage,
With bloody claws growl on the golden stage
Where, while devouring jaws on men they try,

petronius

The people clap to see their fellows die.
But oh! who can without a blush relate
The vicious modes that will destroy the state?
When Persian customs, into fashion grown,
Make nature start and her best work disown;
Male infants are divorced from all that can
By timely progress ripen into man.
Thus circling nature, damped a while, restrains
Her hasty course and in a pause remains.
The herd of fops the frantic humour take,
Each keeps a capon, loves its mincing gait,
Its flowing hair, and striving all it can
In changing mode and dress t' appear a man.
Behold the wilder luxury of Rome!
From Africk furniture, slaves, tables come,
And purple mottled carpets from its loom.
Thus their estates run out while all around
The sot-companions in their wine are drowned.
The soldier loads—neglected is his sword—
With all his spoils the dearly noble board.
Rome's appetite grows witty! And what's caught
In Sicily to its boards is living brought.
To raise our gusts with wanton arts we try
And with expensive sauce new hunger buy.
The Phasian banks, the birds all eaten, gone,
With their forsaken trees in silence moan
And have no music but the winds alone.
In our elections see what frenzies reign,
Where bribed assemblies sell their votes for gain.
Their servile votes obey the chink of gold—
A people and a senate to be sold!
The senate's self, which should our rights defend,
Fawns on the rich and for their interest bend.

The power of right, by gold corrupted, dies
And trampled majesty beneath it lies.
Cato's advice the giddy rout neglect,
But did not him, but him they raised, deject.
Who, though he won, with conscious blushes stands,
Ashamed of power he took from worthier hands.
O manners' ruin and the people's shame!
He suffered not alone, the Roman name,
Virtue and honour, to their period came.
Thus wretched Rome does her own ruin share;
She sells herself, and is herself the ware.
All lands are mortgaged, the whole empire bound,
And in the use the principal is drowned.
Thus debt's a fever and like that disease,
Bred in our bowels, by unfelt degrees
Will through our vitals every member seize.

Fierce tumults now to arms for succour call,
For want may dare but never fear a fall.
Wasted by riot, wealth's a putrid sore
That only wounds can its lost strength restore.
What rules of reason or soft gentle ways
Rome from this lethargy of vice can raise?
When such mild arts can no impression make,
Wars, tumults, noise, and fury must awake.

Fortune one age with three great chiefs supplied
Who by the sword they drew variously died.
On Asia's plains the Parthians Crassus slew
And broke his troops with their revengeful yew;
Great Pompey's blood the Egyptian tyrant shed;
In thankless Rome the murdered Caesar bled.
Thus, as one soil alone too narrow were
Their glorious dust and great remains to bear,
Wide o'er the earth their scattered ruin lies.

petronius

Such honours to the mighty dead arise!
  Betwixt Parthenope and Baia's tide
A cavern lies, most dreadful, deep and wide,
Where runs the raging black Cocytus stream
That from its waters sends a sulphurous steam.
O'er all the fatal compass of its breath
No verdant autumn crowns the fruitful earth,
No blooming woods with vernal songs resound,
Nothing but black confusion all around,
Where lonely rocks in dismal quiet mourn
Which aged cypress dreadfully adorn.
Here Pluto raised his head and through a cloud
Of fire and smoke, in this prophetic mood,
To Fortune spoke: "Great Queen, whose sovereign sway
No less than fate, both Gods and men obey,
You never like what too securely stands;
Does Rome not tire your faint supporting hands?
How can you longer bear her sinking frame
When Roman youth now hate the Roman name?
See! all around luxuriant trophies lie,
And their decreasing wealth new ills supply.
Here golden piles the azure skies invade,
There in the sea encroaching moles are made.
Inverted Nature's injured laws they wrong
And threaten realms which do to me belong.
Such mighty caverns in the earth some make
They threat my empire and my regions shake,
While to low quarries others sink for stone
And hollow rocks beneath their fury groan.
Proud with the hopes to see the light of day
My subject ghosts begin to disobey.
Fortune, arise! stir up the Roman hosts
And fill our desert realms with countless ghosts.

satyricon

Our sooty lips this age no blood have taste,
With thirst Tisiphone's dry throat does waste,
Since Sulla's sword let out the purple flood
And the grim earth grew fruitful from the blood."
  The awful God did thus to Fortune say,
Reaching her hand the yielding earth gave way.
The fickle Goddess thus returning said:
"Father, by all beneath this earth obeyed,
If dangerous truths may be with safety told,
My thoughts with yours a due proportion hold.
No less a rage this willing breast inspires
Nor am I pressed with less inflamed desires.
I curse the blessings that to Rome I lent,
And of my bounty, now abused, repent.
Thus the proud height of Rome's aspiring wall
By the same God that raised it, down shall fall.
I long to see their corpses feed the pires
And in their blood to drown their low desires.
I twice can see Pharsalian armies slain,
The funeral piles of Thessaly and Spain,
Egyptian woes and Libyan groans I hear,
An Actian sea fight and retreating fear.
Fling wide the entrance to your thirsty reign
And summon thither all the countless slain,
Whom Charon's narrow boat will ne'er convey;
Scarce a whole fleet could speed them on their way.
Furies shall be with the vast ruin crowned
And, filled with blood, remangle every wound.
The universal fabric of the world,
Rent and divided, to your Empire's hurled."
  Scarce had she spoke ere from a cloud there flies
A blasting flame that, bursting, shook the skies.
At Jove's fraternal thunder, to his hell,

petronius

Earth closing up, affrighted Pluto fell.
When soon the angry Gods dire omens show
That bode destruction and approaching woe.
Astonishment surprised the darkened sun
As if the war already were begun.
Approaching ills the conscious Cynthia knew
And blushing, from impiety withdrew.
With hideous noise the falling mountains cleave
And streams, repulsed, their usual courses leave.
Engaging armies in the clouds appear
And trumpets calling Mars himself to war.
Now Etna's flames with an unusual roar
Vomit huge bolts of thunder in the air.
Amidst the tombs and bones that lack their urns
Portending spirits set up dismal groans.
A comet's seen with stars unknown before,
And Jove descending in a bloody shower.
Not long the God such wonders dire unfolds.
Caesar no longer his great might withholds;
Impatient of revenge, brooks no delay,
And turns from Gallic wars to civil fray.

   High on the Alps, where the divided rock
To the Greek hero did its nerves unlock,
Altars devoted to Alcides smoke
And Gallic prayers great Hercules invoke.
The temple with eternal ice is crowned,
Whose milky top in hazy clouds is drowned;
You'd think its shoulders in the heavens bound.
The melted snows ne'er from its summits run,
Thawed by the force of a meridian sun.
So fixed with ice and snow it doth appear
That its aspiring top the globe might bear.
Here conquering Caesar leads his joyful bands

And on the proudest cliff considering stands;
The distant plain of Italy surveys
And, hands and voice to heaven directed, prays:
   "Almighty Jove and you, Saturnia, found
Safe by my arms, oft with my triumphs crowned,
Witness these arms unwillingly I wear,
Compelled by injuries too great to bear.
Proscribed and banished whilst I mixed with blood
The conquered Rhine and swelled its angry flood.
When Gauls prepare our Rome to re-invade,
I force to skulk behind their Alps, afraid.
My conquests have my banishment secured,
For sixty triumphs cannot be endured.
Are German conquests reckoned such a fault?
By whom is glory such a monster thought?
A foreign spawn, a mob in arms appear,
At once Rome's scandal and at once her care.
No slavish soul shall bind this arm in chains
And unrevenged contemn my warlike pains.
Bold with success I'll to new conquests lead;
Come, my companions, thus my cause I'll plead:
Let's boldly fight, alike upon us all
Does equal guilt and equal danger call.
With you I fought and conquered, not alone.
Since to be punished is the victor's crown,
Let Fortune judge and let the dice fall down.
My cause is pleaded when you bravely dare:
With such an army, who success can fear?"
   Thus Caesar spoke. From the propitious sky
Descending eagles, boding victory,
Drive the slow winds before them as they fly.
From the left side of a dark wood proceed
Unwonted cries which, dying, flames succeed.

201

petronius

The sunbeams with unusual brightness rise
And spread new glories round the gilded skies.
  New fired with omens of the promised day
Caesar o'er untrod mountains leads the way.
To their advance the frozen earth and snows
Only a dreadful stillness can oppose.
But when the Cuirassiers had broke the chain
And softened milky clouds of frozen rain
So quick the melted snows to rivers run
That soon a deluge from the mountains sprung;
When sudden colds the shuddering currents seize,
Stop their slow streams and rising billows freeze.
The currents, frozen to an icy way,
To sudden falls both men and horse betray.
Now pregnant clouds a gloomy horror form
And, bursting, are delivered of a storm.
Large stones of hail the troubled heavens shoot
That by tempestuous winds are whirled about.
So thick it pours, whole clouds of snow and hail
Like frozen billows on their armour fall.
The earth lay vanquished under mighty snow,
An icy damp the vanquished heavens know,
And vanquished waters now no longer flow.
Caesar alone unvanquished; on his lance
The hero leaning, did secure advance.
Alcmena's son did less securely rush
From the proud height of soaring Caucasus,
Or Jove himself when down the steep he pressed
Those sons of earth that durst his heaven molest.
  While raging Caesar scales th'aspiring height,
Big with the news, Fame takes her feathered flight,
And from Mount Palatine approaching ills
To frighted Rome thus dreadfully she tells:

"A numerous fleet is riding o'er the main,
The melted Alps are hid with Caesar's train,
That reeking from a German conquest come
And with a like destruction threaten Rome."
Now arms, blood, death and dismal scenes of war
Are to each eye presented from afar.
With dreadful thoughts of coming war possessed,
A wilder tumult reigns in every breast.
This flies by land and this the deep explores,
Thinking the sea less dangerous than the shores.
The daring soldier trusts his sword and shield
And boldly runs the hazard of the field.
Fears furnish wings to flight. And—sad to see—
The mobile crowds their empty city flee.
Flight is Rome's joy. And so at Rumour's calls
The vanquished citizens desert their walls.
One takes his children in his trembling arms,
Another keeps his household gods from harms.
Scared from their homes, unwillingly they go,
And in their wishes stab the absent foe.
Their weeping wives uxorious husbands bear;
These guard their parents with a filial care.
The tender youth, unused to burdens, save
Only that with them for which most they crave.
Some, less discreet, strive to bear all away
And only for the foe prepare the prey.
So in a storm, when no sea arts avail
To guide the ship with any certain sail,
Some bind the splitted mast, some swim to shore,
While with full sails kind fortune some implore.
But why do we of vulgar fears complain
When both the consuls did their honour stain?
Great Pompey too his city can forsake;

petronius

That Asia awed, that made Hydaspes quake,
The only rock that did the pirates break,
Whose triumphs thrice made Jove himself afraid
Proud with success he'd next high heaven invade,
To whom the Ocean yielding honours gave,
For whom the Bosphorus humbly stilled its wave—
See! he can quit the greatness of his name
And meanly thus abandon Rome and Fame.
   Now this to Heaven itself does fears impart
And the mild train of quiet Gods depart.
Frighted with wars, they quit the impious world
Leaving mankind in wild confusion hurled.
Fair Peace, as leader of the heavenly train,
Beating her snowy arms did first complain.
A soldier's helmet hid her conquered head
And to Hell's dark insatiate realms she fled.
Justice and Faith on her attending went,
And mournful Concord with her garments rent.
On t'other side from Hell's wide gaping jaws
A train of foul inhabitants arose.
Dreadful Erinys, fierce Bellona dire,
Fraud, and Megaera armed with brands of fire,
The ghastly image of pale Death entire.
Disorder'd Rage from all her fetters freed
Proudly midst these lifts her distracted head.
Her wounded face a bloody helmet hides
And her left arm a battered target guides.
Red brands of fire supported in her right
The impious world with flames and ruin fright.
The Gods descending leave their blest abode.
And wondering Atlas missed his usual load.
For all the inhabitants of Heaven come
Choosing their sides with factious fury down.

satyricon

For Caesar first Dione does appear,
Pallas, and Mars with his huge brandished spear.
Phoebus and Phoebe too for Caesar came
And winged Mercury elects the same.
The trumpets sound, and with a dismal yell
Wild Discord rises from the depths of Hell;
From her swelled eyes there ran a briny flood
And blood congealed o'er all her visage stood;
A filthy gore there issued from her tongue,
With snaky locks her guarded head was hung,
Rent and divided did her garb betray
The image of the breast on which it lay,
And brandished flames her trembling hand obey.
Thus from Hell's deeps she passed with dire design
Up to the top of noble Apennine,
From whose proud height she all the world descried:
Covered with glittering troops on every side,
And bursting out at length with fury, cried:
"Let murd'rous rage to arms the world inspire
And deadly feuds set all mankind on fire.
No age or sex shall from the war be free,
No subtle fear be a security.
The earth itself shall tremble and the shock
Make riven mountains 'gainst each other knock.
Marcellus guide the laws, Curio the crowd,
Let Lentulus inspire the warlike God.
But why is't Caesar such slow measures takes?
Not scale the walls? Nor force the lofty gates?
Nor to the town nor to the treasure makes?
At Rome if Pompey fears the approaching foe
Let him to fatal Epidamnum go.
Fill all its plains with blood." Thus Discord said,
And impious earth her black decrees obeyed.

When Eumolpus with his usual freedom had delivered himself of these lines we arrived at Crotona where, having refreshed ourselves in a little inn we took up at, the next day designing an enlargement of our house and fortune, we fell into the company of some flattering parasites who immediately enquired what we were and whence we came. When, according to our contrivance prudently advancing our characters, we told the credulous knaves from whence we set out and the occasion of our voyage. Upon which, immediately all their fortunes were at Eumolpus's feet, and each, to ingratiate himself into his favour, strove to exceed the rest in presenting him.

While this flood of fortune was for a long time flowing upon us, Eumolpus, midst his happiness, having lost the memory of his former condition, so boasted his interest that he affirmed none in Crotona could resist his desires, and that whatever crime any of us should be guilty of, he had friends potent enough to secure us from punishment. But though our daily increasing riches left my pampered body no desire unsatisfied, and though I flattered myself into an opinion that ill fortune had taken her last leave of me, yet not only the thoughts of my present condition but the means of getting to it would often break in upon my joys and embitter all the sweet. "And what," said I to myself, "if some one wiser than the rest should dispatch a messenger for Africk, should we not soon be discovered? What if the servant of Eumolpus, glutted with his present happiness, should betray us to his companions and maliciously discover the whole cheat? We should then be put upon the stroll again and be obliged with shame to renew our former beggary. Heavens, how ill it fares with wicked livers! They ever expect the punishment they deserve!"

«Going out full of these thoughts, to divert my concern, I resolved on a walk, but I had scarce got into a public one ere a pretty girl made up to me and, calling me Polyaenus, told me her lady would be proud of an opportunity to speak with me. "You're mistaken, sweetheart," returned I in a little heat. "I'm but a servant, of another country too, and not worthy of so great a favour." "No, sir," said she, "I have commands to you,» but because you know what you can do, you're proud, and if a lady would receive a favour from you I see she must buy it. For to what end are all those allurements, forsooth—the curled hair, the complexion advanced by washes, the wanton roll of your eyes, the affected air of your gait, the mincing steps—unless, by showing your parts, to invite a purchaser? For my part I am neither witch nor conjurer, yet can guess at a man by his physiognomy and, when I find a spark walking, can guess the meaning. To be short, sir, if so be you are one of them that sell their ware I'll procure you a buyer, but if you are a courteous lender, confer the benefit. As for your being a servant and below, as you say, such a favour, it increases the flames of her that's dying for you. 'Tis the foolish humour of some women to be in love with filth, nor can they be raised to an appetite but by the charms, forsooth, of some slave or lackey. Some can be pleased with nothing but a prize-fighter, or a muleteer smothered in dust, or an actor incited to prostitute himself on the stage by the vanity of showing his pretty shapes there. Of this sort is my lady, who indeed pre-

fers the paltry lover of the upper gallery, with his dirty face and oaken staff, to all the fine gentlemen in the boxes with their patches, gunpowder spots, and tooth-pickers."

When, pleased with the humour of her talk, "I beseech you, child," said I, "are you the she that's so in love with my person?" Upon which the maid fell into a fit of laughing. "I would not," returned she, "have you so extremely flatter yourself. I never yet truckled to a slave nor will Venus allow I should embrace a gibbet. You must address yourself to ladies that kiss the marks of the lash. Be assured that I, though a slave, have too fine a taste to converse with any below a knight." I was amazed at the relation of such unequal passions and thought it miraculous to find a servant with the scornful pride of a lady and a lady with the humility of a servant.

Our pleasant discourse continuing, I desired her to bring her lady to the mall of plane trees. She readily consented and, taking hold of her petticoats, tripped it gently into a laurel labyrinth that bordered on the walk. 'Twas not long ere she ushered her lady to me and I found at my side a beauty excelling even the flattery of painters; words can't express so perfect a creature, whatever I should say of her would fall short of what she was. Her hair spread all over her shoulders and seemed in easy curls to wanton in the air. A tiny forehead naturally inclined the hair to its advantage. Her eyebrows declined to the outline of her cheeks and almost crossed on the line of her nose. Her eyes eclipsed the glory of the brightest star. Her nostrils had an easy turn and her mouth was such as Praxiteles believed Diana had. Then her chin, her neck, her hands, her feet gently girt with golden sandals to whose whiteness the Parian marble would serve but as a foil. 'Twas then I began to despise my old mistress, Doris, and thus broke out:

"Sure amorous Jove's a holy tale above,
With fancied arts that wait upon his love.
When we are blest with such a charm as this,
And he no rival to our happiness,
How well the bull would now the God become
Or his grey hairs to be transformed to down.
Here's Danae's self. A touch from her would fire
And make the God in liquid joys expire."

She was pleased and smiled with such an air that she seemed like the moon in her silver glories breaking through a cloud. When, addressing herself, her pretty fingers humouring the turn of her voice, "If a fine woman, and that but this year has been acquainted with man," said she, "may deserve your love, let me offer you a mistress. I am sensible you have a comrade already, nor have I thought it below me to make enquiries. But why not a mistress too? I enter the list on the same bottom with your friend. Nor do I desire to engross all your caresses; only think me deserving and confer them as you please."

"Let me beseech you, Madam," returned I, "by all those Cupids in your face and mien, not to scorn to admit a stranger into the number of your devotees. You'll find him most religious if you accept his devotions, and that you should not suspect I believe the way to this heaven may be trod gratis, I offer up to you my comrade."

"What?" said she, "You offer me him without whom you cannot live? On whose lips your very being hangs!

Whom you so love as I could you!" Her words were attended with such a grace at their delivery and the sweet sound so charmed the yielding air you would have sworn some syren had been breathing melodies. Thus rapt with everything to amazing and fancying a glory shined in every part, I ventured to enquire what name the goddess owned. "So," said she, "my maid has not informed you I am called Circe? I would not have you believe, though I bear that name, that I derive my origin from the Sun God nor that my mother, while she lay in the god's embraces, halted the motions of the firmament. Yet I shall be god-like enough if fate will give you to my arms. Though we know it not, some God is here at work. Not without reason does Circe love Polyaenus; these two names have ever kindled a mighty flame. Therefore come, my dear, and crown my wishes. Nor need you fear any malicious disturber of our joys; your comrade is far enough from hence." Upon which she threw her downy arms about me and led me to a plot of ground, the pride of nature, decked with a gay variety of every pleasing flower.

> On Ida's top when Jove his nymph caressed
> And lawless heat in open view expressed,
> His mother earth in all her charms was seen,
> The rose, the violet, the sweet jessamine,
> And the fair lily smiling on the green.
> Such was the plot on which my Venus lay;
> Our love was secret, but the charming day
> Was bright, like her, and as her temper, gay.

Here we prepared for battle and through ten thousand kisses pressed to a closer engagement, but a sudden weakness robbed me of my arms. «Thus cheated in her expectations, she highly resenting it,» "What is this?" said she. "Do my kisses offend thee? Or my breath, heavy through fasting? Or the ill scent of my armpits? Or if none of these, dost thou fear Gito?" I was so ashamed of myself that if there was any spark of the man left in me I lost it. And, finding every part of me feeble and as it were lifeless, "I beseech you, Madam," said I, "don't triumph over my misery. I'm certainly bewitched!"

«So slight an excuse could not allay her resentment but, giving me a disdainful glance, she turned to her maid:» "Tell me, Chrysis, the truth. Is there anything misbecoming or ungenteel about me? Or have I used art to hide any natural deformity? Do not deceive your mistress. I must have some defect; what is it?" Upon which, ere Chrysis could make a return, she snatched a pocket glass from her and after she had practised all those looks that usually excite love, she took hold of her petticoats that were a little rumpled with lying on, and immediately ran to a neighbouring temple dedicated to Venus. Like a condemned criminal and trembling as from a horrid dream I began to consider whether I had been robbed of any real joy.

> So when a dream our sleeping sight betrays
> And to our view some hidden gold conveys,
> Our busy hands the inviting treasure seize

And short lived joys our active fancies please.
But soon we fear lest any conscious spy
May find the secret and the theft decry.
And when with spleen our charming dreams are o'er,
Our minds restored to what they were before,
Concerned, we wish the fancied loss regained
And with the image still are entertained.

«This misfortune might make me justly think it not only a true vision but real witchcraft, for I was so weak I could scarce get on my legs. My mind at last, a little freed, began by degrees to recover its vigour, upon which I went to my lodging and, dissembling a faintness, lay down on my bed. A little after, Gito, being informed I was ill, came to me much troubled, but to allay his concern I told him I was only a little weary and had a mind for a nap, but not a word of my last adventure. I talked to him about several things but was afraid to disclose the secret because I knew he envied everyone that appeared agreeable to me. And to prevent his suspicion, throwing my arms about him, I endeavoured to give a proof of my love, but, disappointed of the expectation I had raised him to, he rose, very angry, from my side and, accusing my weakness and strange behaviour to him, told me that of late he had found my chief favours were bestowed in another's arms. "My love for you, Gito," said I, "has ever been the same, but now my dancing days submit to reason." Gito, laughing, replied:» "I give you therefore a thousand thanks that you love me with more than Platonic discretion.

Alcibiades never lay more virginally in the bed of Socrates!" "Then," added I, "believe me, Gito. I hardly know I've anything of man about me. How useless lies the terrible part where I was once Achilles!" «When he found how unfit I was to confer the favours he wanted,» to prevent suspicion of his privacy with me, he jumped up and ran to another part of the house.

«He was hardly gone ere Chrysis entered my chamber and gave me a billet from her mistress in which I found this written:» "Circe to Polyaenus. Had I flattered myself with an expectation of pleasure I might complain that I have been deceived. Now I'm obliged to your impotence that has made me sensible how much too long I have trifled with mistaken hopes of satisfaction. But pray, sir, how do you design to bestow yourself? Did you rashly venture home on your own legs? For no physician ever allowed that men could walk without strength. Let me advise your tender years to beware of a palsy; I never saw anybody in such danger before. Part of you is dead already and should the same chillness seize you all over you can prepare your funeral. What is to be done? Even after receiving such an affront I shall not envy the cure of a weak unhappy wretch. If you would recover your strength, ask Gito, or rather not ask him for it. I can assure you a return of your vigour if you could sleep three nights alone. As to myself I am not in the least apprehensive of appearing to another less charming than I have to you. I am told neither my glass nor report do flatter me. Farewell if you can."

When Chrysis found I had read the reproach, "Such mischances," said she, "are not rare, and chiefly in this city where women are so potent in magic charms even to make the moon confess their power. Therefore, the recovery of any useful instrument of love becomes their care. 'Tis only writing some soft tender things to my lady and you make her happy. For 'tis confessed since her disappointment she has not been herself."

I readily consented and calling for paper, thus addressed myself: "Polyaenus to Circe. 'Tis confessed, Madam, I have often sinned, for I am not only a man but a very young one, yet never left the field so dishonourably before. You have at your feet a confessing criminal that deserves whatever you can inflict. I've cut a throat, betrayed my country, committed sacrilege; if a punishment for any of these will serve, I am ready to receive sentence. If you fancy my death, I wait on you with my sword. But if a beating will content you, I fly naked to your arms. Only remember 'twas not the workman but his instruments that failed. I was ready to engage but wanted arms. Who robbed me of them I know not. Perhaps my eager mind outran my body, or while with an unhappy haste I aimed at all, I was cheated with abortive joys. I only know I don't know what I've done. You bid me fear a palsy as if the disease could do more that has already robbed me of that by which I should have purchased you. All I have to say for myself is this: that I will certainly pay with interest the arrears of love if you allow me to repair my misfortune."

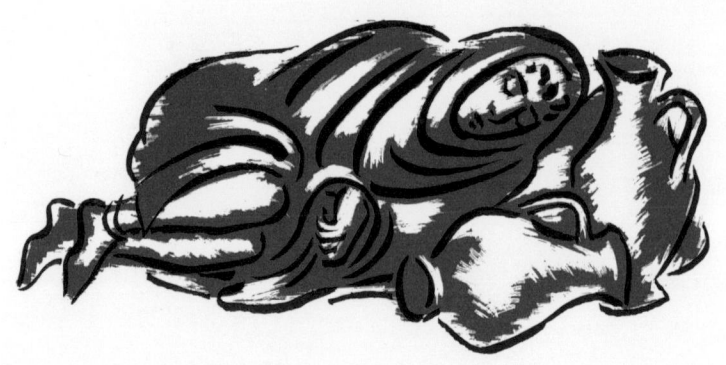

Having sent back Chrysis with this answer, to encourage my jaded body, after the bath and strengthening oils had a little raised me, I betook myself to such a course of diet as might render me strong and vigorous, such as onions and braised snails without sauce, using wine very moderately. Upon which, to settle myself, I took a little walk and, returning to my chamber, slept that night without Gito. So great was my care to acquit myself honourably with my mistress that I was afraid of any temptation which might have drawn me from my duty.

The next day, rising without prejudice either to my body or spirits, I went, though I feared the place was ominous, to the same copse, and among the trees waited for Chrysis to conduct her mistress. I had not been long there ere she came to me and with her a little old woman. After she had saluted me, "What, my nice Sir Courtly," said she, "does your stomach begin to come to you?" At what time the old woman, drawing from her bosom a ribbon of many colours, bound my neck and having mixed spittle and dust she dipped her finger in it and marked my forehead, whether I would or no. When this part of the charm was over, she made me spit thrice and as often put into my bosom enchanted stones that she had wrapped in purple. After which, she began to examine my breeches when, quick as thought, the swelling inhabitant obeyed her power and filled her hands with his motion. She was all joy and, "D'ye see, my Chrysis," said she, "what a hare I have started for another to have the pleasure of the chase?

> Never despair: Priapus I invoke
> To help the parts that make his altars smoke."

«After this the old woman presented me to Chrysis, who was very glad she had recovered her mistress's treasure, and therefore, hastening to her, she conducted me to a most pleasant retreat decked with all that nature could produce to please the sight.»

> Where lofty planes cast a refreshing shade
> And well trimmed pines their shaking tops displayed,
> Where Daphne midst the cypress crowned her head,
> Near these a circling river gently flows
> And rolls the pebbles as it murmuring goes.
> A Place designed for love. The nightingale
> And other birds its soft delights can tell,
> That on each bush salute the coming day
> And in their orgies sing its hours away.

She was in an undress, resting her marble neck on a golden pillow and diverting herself with a myrtle branch. As soon as I appeared she blushed, as mindful of her disappointment. The maids very prudently withdrew and when we were left together I approached the temptation. At what time she screened my face with the

myrtle and, as if there had been a wall between us, becoming more bold, "What, my cold spark?" said she, "Have you brought all yourself to-day?" "Do you ask, Madam," I returned, "rather than try?" And, throwing myself to her that with open arms was eager to receive me, I enjoyed to the full kisses free from witchcraft, when, giving the signal to prepare for other joys, she drew me to a more close embrace. And now our murmuring kisses their sweetness tell; now our twining limbs tried each fold of love; now, locked in each other's arms, our bodies and our souls are joined. «But even here, alas! even amidst these sweet beginnings, a sudden chillness pressed upon my joys and made me leave them all imperfect.»

Circe, enraged to be so affronted, had recourse to revenge and, calling the grooms that belonged to the house, made them give me a flogging. Nor was she satisfied with this, but calling all the servant wenches, even the meanest in the house, she made 'em spit on me. I hid my head as well as I could and, without begging pardon, for I knew what I had deserved, was turned out of doors with a large retinue of kicks and spittle. Proselenos, the old woman, was turned out too, and Chrysis beaten, and the whole household wondering with themselves enquired the cause of their lady's disorder.

I hid my bruises as well as I could lest my rival Eumolpus might sport with my shame or Gito be concerned at it. Therefore, as the only way to disguise my misfortune I began to dissemble sickness and, having got in bed, to revenge myself of that part of me that had been the cause of all my misfortune.

> With dreadful steel the part I would have lopped,
> Thrice from my trembling hand the razor dropped.
> Now, what I might before, I could not do
> For, cold as ice, the fearful thing withdrew
> And shrunk behind a wrinkled canopy,
> Hiding his head from my revenge and me.
> Thus by his fear I'm baulked of my design
> And must in words more killing vent my spleen.

At what time, raising myself on the bed in this or like manner, I reproached the sullen impotent: "With what face can you look up, thou shame of heaven and man that can'st not be seriously mentioned? Have I deserved from you when raised within sight of the heaven of joys to be struck down to the lowest hell? To have a scandal fixed on the very prime and vigour of my years and to be reduced to the weakness of an old man? I beseech you, sir, give me an epitaph on my departed vigour." Though in a great heat I had thus said,

> He still continued looking on the ground,
> Nor more, at this, had raised his guilty head
> Than withered poppies on their tender stalks.

Nor when I had done, did I less repent of my ridiculous passion, and with a conscious blush began to think how unaccountable it was that, forgetting all shame, I should contend with that part of me that all men of sense reckon not worth their thoughts. But after I had struck my forehead many a time, "But what's the crime," began I, "if by a natural complaint I was eased of my grief? Or how is it that we so often curse our bellies or our mouths or heads when they are distempered? What? Did not Ulysses argue with his heart? And do we not hear tragic heroes blame their eyes as though they could hear the play? Those that have gout in their legs swear at them; those that have it in their fingers do so by them; those that have sore eyes are angry with their eyes.

> Why do the solemn coxcombs of the age
> At my familiar lines unjustly rage?
> In measures loosely plain blunt satyre flows
> And all that people do sincerely shows.
> Love I describe and all the wanton joys
> Of blushing matrons and of amorous boys.
> Such bliss wise Epicurus did commend
> And of our life called this the right true end.

There's nothing more deceitful than a ridiculous opinion nor more ridiculous than an affected gravity."

After this I called Gito to me and, "Tell me," said I, "but sincerely, whether Ascyltos when he took you from me pursued the injury that night or was chastely content to lie alone?" The boy, with his finger in his eyes, took a solemn oath that he had no incivility offered him by Ascyltos.

«This drove me to my wits end, nor did I well know what to say. "For why," I considered, "should I think of the twice mischievous accident that lately befell me?" At last I did what I could to recover my vigour and, being willing to invoke the assistance of the Gods, I went out to pay my devotions to Priapus and, as wretched as I was, I did not despair but,» kneeling at the entry of the chamber, thus besought the hostile god:

"Bacchus and Nymphs delight, O mighty God,
Whom Cynthia gave to rule the blooming wood,
Lesbos and verdant Thasos thee adore
And Lydians rich in seven great streams implore
And raise devoted temples to thy power!
Thou Dryad's joy and Bacchus's guardian, hear
My conscious prayer with an attentive ear.
My hands with guiltless blood I never stained,
Or sacrilegiously the gods profaned.
To feeble me restoring blessings send,
I did not thee with my whole self offend.
Who sins through weakness is less guilty thought;
Be pacified and spare a venial fault.
On me when fate shall smiling gifts bestow

petronius

I'll not ungrateful to thy godhead go.
A destined goat shall on thy altar lie
And the horned parent of my flock shall die.
A sucking pig I'll offer to thy shrine
And sacred bowls brim-full of generous wine.
Then thrice thy frantic votaries shall round
Thy temple dance, with smiling garlands crowned
And most devoutly drunk, thy orgies sound."

While I was thus praying and keeping a careful watch on my lifeless member, an old woman, with her hair about her ears and disfigured with a mournful habit, came into the temple and, taking hold of me, drew me out of the entry. "What hag," said she, "has devoured your manhood? Or what ominous carcass have you stumbled over in your nightly walks? You have not acquitted your self above a boy but, faint, weak, and tired, like a horse overcharged in a steep, have lost your toil and sweat. Nor content to sin alone but have provoked the offended gods against me."

When leading me, obedient to all her commands, a second time to the cell of a neighbouring priestess of Priapus, she threw me upon the bed and, taking up the broom from behind the door, began to beat me. I very patiently received her fury and, if the breaking of the stick at the first stroke had not lessened its force, she might have broke my head and arms. I groaned and, hiding my face with my hands in a flood of tears, leaned on the pillow. The old woman sat down beside me and wept as bitterly as myself complaining shrilly of the miseries of old age till the priestess came in upon us and, "What," said she, "do you do in my chapel as melancholy as if you came from a funeral? This is a holiday in which even the mournful are merry." "Alas! My Oenothea," said she, "this youth you see here was born under an ill star, for neither boy nor maid can raise him to a perfect appetite. You ne'er beheld a more unhappy man! In his garden the weak willow, not the lusty cedar, grows. In short, you may guess what he is that could rise unblest from Circe's bed." Upon this, Oenothea set herself between us and, moving her head a while, "I," said she, "am the only one that can give a remedy for that disease and, not to delay it, let him sleep with me tonight, and next morning examine how vigorous I shall have made him.

All nature's works my magic powers obey:
The blooming earth shall wither and decay
And, when I please, be verdant, fresh, and gay.
From rugged rocks I make sweet waters flow
And raging billows to me humbly bow,
While rivers, winds, when I command, obey
And at my feet their useless fans will lay.
Tigers and pards, submissive to my will,
Obey my orders and neglect to kill.
But these are small when of my magic verse
The moon in falling doth the power confess;
When my commands make trembling Phoebus rein
His fiery steeds, then journey back again.
Such power have charms, by whose prevailing aid
The fury of the raging bulls was laid.
The heaven-born Circe with her magic song
Ulysses's men did into monsters turn.
Proteus, by them, assumed what shape he would.
I who this art so long have understood
Can send proud Ida's top into the main
And make the billows bear it up again."

I shook with fear at such a romantic promise and began more attentively to view the old woman. . . . "Therefore," Oenothea cried out, "obey my power!" when, carefully wiping her hands, she lay down on the bed and half smothered me with kisses. . . .

Oenothea in the middle of the altar placed a turf table which she heaped with burning coals and an old cracked cup, repaired with pitch, which she used for sacrifice. In taking down the cup she drew out the nail on which it was hanging and had to thrust it back into the smoky wall. Then, putting on her habit, she placed a huge kettle by the fire and with a fork took down a bag that hung in the meat pantry in which were her provision of beans and a very aged piece of a hog's forehead with the print of a hundred cuts on it. When, opening the bag, she threw me a part of the beans and bid me carefully strip them. I obey her command and try with cunning fingers to strip the beans from their nasty coverings, but she, blaming my dullness, snatched them from me and skillfully tearing the shells with her teeth spat the black morsels from her, that lay like dead flies on the ground. How ingenious is poverty and what strange arts will hunger teach!

> Here shines no glittering ivory set with gold,
> No marble covers the well-trodden mould
> By its own wealth deluded; but the shrine
> With simple modest ornaments doth shine.
> Round Ceres' bower the bending osier grows,
> Earthen is all the plate the priestess knows.
> No brazen knobs nor splendid purple pride,
> Mud mixed with straw the pious relics hide.
> With rush and reed is thatched the hut itself,
> Where, besides what is on a smoky shelf,
> Ripe service-berries into garlands bound
> And savory bunches with dried grapes are found.
> Such a low cottage Hecale confined;
> Low was her cottage but sublime her mind.
> Her bounteous heart a grateful praise shall crown
> And muses make immortal her renown.

petronius

After which, she tasted a little of the flesh and hanging the rest, old as herself, on the nail, the rotten stool on which she was mounted, breaking, threw her into the fire. Her fall broke the kettle and that put out the fire that was beginning to take. She burnt her elbow and all her face was hid with the ashes that her fall had raised. Thus disturbed, I arose and took her up. Immediately, lest anything should hinder the sacrifice, she ran for new fire to the neighbours. . . . So I advanced to the door of the cottage. . . .

When behold! I was set upon by three sacred geese that daily, I believe, about that time, were fed by the old woman. They made a hideous noise and, surrounding me, one tears my coat, another my shoes, while their furious captain made a very brisk attack on my legs. Till, seeing myself in danger, I began to be in earnest and, snatching up one of the feet of our little table, made the valiant animal feel the weight of my armed hand. Nor content with a slight blow or two, I revenged myself with its death.

> Such were the birds Alcides did subdue
> That from his conquering arm to heaven withdrew.
> Such sure the Harpies were which poison strewed
> On cheated Phineus's false deluding food.
> Loud lamentations shake the trembling air;
> The powers above the wild confusion share.
> Horrors disturb the order of the sky
> And frighted stars beyond their courses fly.

By this time the other two had eat up the beans that

lay scattered on the floor and, having lost their leader, returned to the temple. Glad of the booty and my revenge I threw the slain goose behind the bed and cured the slight wound in my leg with vinegar. But, fearing the old woman's anger, I designed to make off and, taking up my clothes, started to leave the cottage. Nor had I reached the door ere I saw Oenothea bringing in her hand an earthen pot filled with burning charcoal. Upon which I retreated and, throwing down my clothes, fixed myself in the entry as if I were impatiently expecting her coming.

Oenothea, entering, placed the borrowed embers on some broken sticks and having heaped more wood upon those began to excuse her stay, that her friend would not let her go before she had, according to the laws of drinking, taken off three healths together. "And now what," said she, "have you been doing in my absence? And where are my beans?" I, who thought I had behaved myself very honourably, told her the whole fight and to end her grief for the loss of the beans presented her the goose. When I showed her the goose the old woman set up such an outcry that you would have thought the geese were re-entering the place. In confusion, and amazed at so strange a humour, I asked the meaning of her passion and why she pitied the goose rather than me.

But wringing her hands, "You wicked wretch," said she, "d'ye dare even to talk? D'ye know what you've done? You've killed the delight of Priapus, a goose the pleasure of all matrons. And lest you should think you've done little harm, know if a magistrate should hear of it you'd be crucified. You have defiled with blood my cell that to this day had been inviolate. You have done that for which, if any's so malicious, he may expel me from my office."

> She said, and trembling rends her aged hairs
> And both her cheeks with wilder fury tears,
> Sad murmurs from her troubled breast arise,
> A shower of tears there issued from her eyes,
> And down her face a rapid deluge run,
> Such as is seen when a hill's frosty crown
> By warm Favonius is melted down.

Upon which, "I beseech you," said I, "don't grieve. I'll recompense the loss of your goose with an ostrich!" While, amazed, I spoke, she sat down on the bed lamenting her loss. At what time Proselenos came in with the sacrifice and, viewing the murdered goose, began very earnestly to cry and pity me as if it had been my father I had slain and not a goose that was public property. But tired with all this stuff, "I beseech you," said I, "tell me, though I had injured you, though it had been a man I killed, won't gold wipe off the guilt? See here are two pieces of gold; with these you may purchase Gods as well as geese." Which when Oenothea beheld, "Pardon me, young man," said she, "I am only concerned for your safety, which is an argument of love, not hatred. Therefore we'll take what care we can to prevent a discovery. You have nothing to do but to entreat the Gods to forgive the sin."

Whoe'er has money may securely sail,
On all things with almighty gold prevail;
May Danae wed or rival amorous Jove
And make her father pander to his love;
May be a poet, preacher, lawyer too,
And, bawling, win the cause he does not know
And up to Cato's fame for wisdom grow.
Wealth without law will gain at bar renown:
Howe'er the case appears the cause is won.
Every rich lawyer is a Littleton.
In short, of all you wish you are possessed;
All things promote the wealthy man's request,
For Jove himself's the master of his chest.

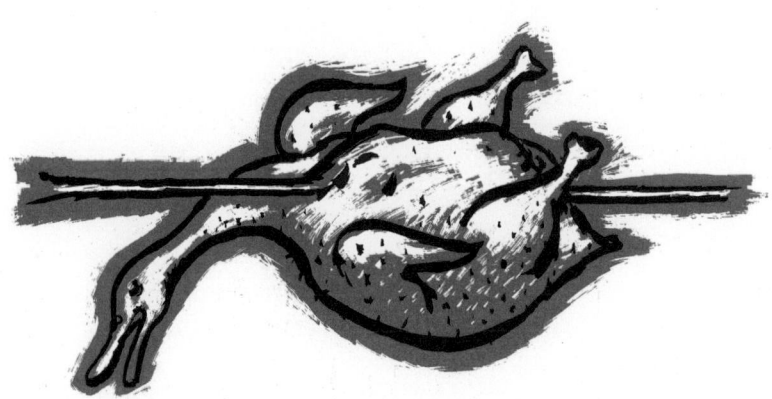

«While my thoughts were thus engaged» she placed a cup of wine under my hands and having cleansed my profane extended fingers with leeks and parsley she threw some hazel nuts into the wine, with a prayer, and as they sunk or swam gave her prognostications. But I well knew the empty rotten ones would swim and those whose kernels were whole would go to the bottom.

Then, applying herself to the goose from its opened breast, she drew a lusty liver, from which she told me my future fortune. And that no mark of the murder might be left, she fixed the cut up goose on a spit and made ready a fine repast for him whom, as she herself confessed, she had but now condemned to death. In the meantime the wine went briskly round «and now the old women gladly ate up the goose they so lately lamented. When they had picked its bones Oenothea, half drunk, turned to me. "And now," said she, "I'll finish the charm that recovers your strength."» When, drawing out a leathern ensign of Priapus, she dipped it in a medley of oil, small pepper and the bruised seed of nettles and began by degrees to direct its passage through my hinder parts. With this mixture she barbarously sprinkled my manhood and, with the juices of cresses and southernwood washing the plat around it, began with a bunch of green nettles to strike gently all the vale below my navel. «Upon which, jumping from her to avoid the sting, I made off. The old woman in a great rage pursued me» and, though drunk with wine and their more hot desires, took the right way and followed me down two or three lanes crying "Stop thief!" But with my toes all bloody in my hasty flight I got off.

«When I got home I went to bed to ease my wearied limbs, but the thoughts of my misfortunes would not let me sleep, when, considering what an unparalleled wretch I was, I cried out: "Did my ever cruel fortune want the afflictions of love to make me more miserable?

O unhappiness! Fortune and love conspire to my ruin. Severer love spares me no way, or loving, or beloved, a wretch. Chrysis adores me and is ever giving me occasion to oblige her. She that when she brought me to her mistress despised me for my mean habit as one beneath her desires,» that very Chrysis that so scorned my former fortune, pursues me now even to the hazard of her own, «and swore, when she first discovered to me the violence of her love, that she would ever be true to me. But Circe's in possession of my heart, I value none but her, and indeed who wears such charms?» Compared to her, what was Ariadne or Leda? What Helen or even Venus? Paris himself, the umpire of the wanton deities, if with these eyes he had seen her contending for the golden apple would have given his Helen and the three goddesses for her. If I might be admitted to kiss her sweet lips again or once more press her divinely rising breasts, perhaps my vigour would revive, which now I believe lies oppressed by witchcraft. I should dispense with my reproaches, should forget I was beat, esteem my being turned out of doors a sport, so I might be again happy in her favours."

«These thoughts and the image of the beautiful Circe so raised my mind that I oft,» as if my love was in my arms, with a great deal of fruitless ardour hugged the bedclothes «till, out of patience with my lasting affliction, I began to reproach my impotence. Yet recovering my presence of mind, I flew for comfort to the misfortunes of ancient heroes and thus broke out:»

Not me alone th' avenging gods pursue;
Oft they their anger on their heroes throw.
By Juno's rage the Heavens Alcides bore
And Pelias injured Juno knew before.
Laomedon Heaven's dire resentments felt
And two gods punished Telephus's guilt.
We cannot from the wrathful godhead run;
Crafty Ulysses could not Neptune shun.
Provoked Priapus over land and sea
Has left the Hellespont to follow me.

«Full of anxious cares I spent the night and Gito, being informed I lay at home, entered my chamber by day break, when, having passionately complained of my loose life, he told me the family took much notice of my behaviour, that I was seldom in waiting, and that perhaps the company I kept would be my ruin. By this I understood he was informed of my affairs and that someone had been in pursuit of me.» Upon which I asked my Gito whether anybody was to enquire for me. "Not this day," said he, "but yesterday there came a very pretty woman who, when she had tired me with a long sifting discourse, at last told me you deserved punishment and would receive that of slaves if the injured party pressed the action."

«This so sensibly touched me that I began afresh to reproach fortune,» nor had I done ere Chrysis came in and, wildly throwing her arms about me, "Now," said she, "I'll hold my wish. You're my love, my joy; nor can you think to quench this flame but by closer embraces." «I was much disturbed at Chrysis's wantonness

and gave her fair language to get rid of her. For I was very apprehensive of the danger of Eumolpus's hearing it, since his good fortune had made him so proud. I did, therefore, what I could to appease her rage. I dissembled love, whispered soft things, and in short managed it so like a lover that she believed me one. I made her understand in what danger we both were if she should be found with me in that place, and that our Lord Eumolpus punished the least offence. Upon which she immediately made out, and the more hastily because she saw Gito returning, who had left me a little before she came.

She was scarce out when» on a sudden, one of the slaves came to me and told me that our lord so highly resented my two days absence that unless, as he advised me, I invented a good excuse to allay his heat I should certainly be punished. «Gito, perceiving how concerned I was, spoke not a word of the woman but advised me to behave myself merrily to Eumolpus, rather than serious. I pursued the counsel and put on so pleasant a face that he received me in drollery without the grave stiffness of a master. He was pleasant on the subject of my amours, praised my mien and wit that was so agreeable to the ladies and, "I'm no stranger," said he, "to your love of a very beautiful lady. But now, Encolpius, that, rightly managed, may turn to our advantage. Therefore do you personate the lover, I'll continue the character I've begun."

He was yet speaking when there entered the room» a very venerable matron, her name Philomela, who by the well-managed virtues of her sex had often got great booties and now, grown old and past her blooming years, she would thrust her son and daughter upon childless old men and thus continue her device. She therefore comes to Eumolpus and commends her children to his conduct; that herself and all her hopes she committed to his wisdom; that he was the only one in this world that with useful precepts could daily inform the minds of young people. In short, she would leave her children there to hear his wisdom, which was the only portion she could give them. Nor was she worse than her word; and leaving a very beautiful girl with her little brother, went out under pretence of paying heaven public thanks in the temple for what she had received.

Eumolpus, to whom I myself seemed but a Ganymede, immediately invited the girl to sacrifice to Priapus. But having reported himself to be gouty and feeble, it might endanger his fortune to alter his character. Therefore, to maintain his pretence, he entreated the girl to savour his belauded conduct by getting uppermost. He then ordered his servant, Corax, to get under the bed so that, placing his hands on the ground, with his body he might move him up and down. He obeyed and with a slow, just motion kept time with the girl above. But when the business was coming to an issue, Eumolpus loudly called to Corax to quicken his strokes, and thus, placed between his mistress and his servant, he seemed to be playing at see-saw. Pleased with the conceit, he often repeated his humour. And I, too, fearing my virtues might rust by disuse, while the boy was admiring his sister's moving engine, advanced to try whether he, too, would be patient in love. The discreet youth did not reject the invitation, but my adverse fortune still attended me.

«I was not so concerned at this as the former, for a little while after, my strength returned, and finding myself more vigorous I cried out:» "Great indeed are the Gods that have made me whole again! For Mercury, that conveys and reconveys our souls, by his favours has restored what his anger had seized. Now I shall be in as great esteem as Protesilaus or any of the ancient heroes."

Upon which, taking up my clothes, I showed my whole self to Eumolpus, who was startled at first, but soon, to confirm his belief, with both hands chafed the mighty favour of the Gods.

«This great blessing making us merry, we laughed at Philomela's cunning and her children's experience in the art, which would profit them little with us, for to no other end were they left but to be heirs to what we had. When reflecting on this sordid manner of deceiving childless age, we took occasion to consider the condition of our present fortune, and Eumolpus declared that the deceivers might be deceived and therefore all our actions should be of a piece with the character we bore.» "Socrates, the wisest of men, used to boast he never saw a tavern nor ever had been in the common company that frequents such places. Nothing is more convenient than a discreet behaviour." "All these are truths," said I, "nor should any sort of men more expect the sudden assaults of ill fortune than those that covet what's other men's. But how should pick-pockets live unless, by some well ordered trick to draw fools together, they get employment? As fish are taken with what they really eat, so men are to be cheated with something that's solid—not empty hopes. «Thus the people of this country have hitherto received us very nobly, but when they find» the arrival of no ship from Africa laden, as you told them, with riches and your retinue, the impatient deceivers will lessen their bounty. Therefore, or I'm mistaken, Fortune begins to repent of her favours to us."

«"I have thought of a means," said Eumolpus, "to make our deceivers continue their care of us." And drawing his will out of his purse he read the last lines of it:» "All that have legacies in this my last will and testament, except my freedmen, receives them on this condition: that they divide my body and eat it before the people. «And that they may not think it an unjust demand, let them know that» to this day 'tis the custom of many countries that the relations of the dead devour the carcasses, and for that reason they often quarrel with their sick kindred because they spoil their flesh by lingering in a disease. I only instance this to my friends that they may not refuse to perform my will, but with the same sincerity they wished well to my soul they might devour my body."

«When he had read the chief articles, some that were more intimately acquainted with him entered the chamber and, viewing the will, earnestly entreated him to impart the contents of it. He readily consented and read the whole. But when they heard the necessity of eating his carcass they seemed much concerned at the strange proposal» but their insatiate love of the money made them stifle their passion «and his person was so awful to them they durst not complain. But one of them, by name» Gorgias, briskly said he was willing to accept the conditions «so he might not wait for the body.

To this Eumolpus replied:» "I'm not in the least apprehensive of your performance nor that your stomach would refuse the task, when to recompense one distaste-

ful minute you may promise yourself ages of luxury.
'Tis but shutting your eyes and supposing instead of a
man's flesh you were eating a million. Some sauce may
be added to vary the taste, for no flesh pleases alone but
is prepared by art to commend it to the stomach. If you
desire instances of this kind to make you approve my
advice, the Saguntines, when they were besieged by
Hannibal, ate human bodies without the hopes of an
estate for doing it. The Petelini, reduced to the last ex-
tremity by famine, did the like, nor had they further
hopes in this banquet than to satisfy nature. When
Scipio took Numantia, mothers were found with their
children half eaten in their arms. «But since the thoughts
only of eating man's flesh create the loathing, 'tis but
resolving and you gain the mighty legacies I leave you."

Eumolpus recounted these shameless inhumanities
with so much confusion that his parasites began to sus-
pect him and, more nearly considering our words and
actions, their jealousy increased with their observation
and they believed us perfect cheats. Upon which, those
that had received us most nobly resolved to seize us and
justly take their revenge, but Chrysis, privy to all strata-
gems, gave me notice of their designs. The frightful
news so struck me that I made off with Gito immedi-
ately and left Eumolpus to the mercy of his enemies.
And in a few days we heard the Crotonians, angry that
that old rascal should have lived so long at such a sump-
tuous rate on the public charge, had sacrificed him the
Massilian way.» Whenever the Massilians were visited

with a plague, someone of the poorest of the people, for the sake of being well fed a whole year at the public charge, would offer himself a sacrifice to appease the Gods. He, after his year was up, dressed in holy wreath and sacred garments, was led about the city with invocations on the Gods that all the sins of the nation might be punished in him, and so was thrown from a precipice.

GLOSSARY

advertised: Informed, notified.

antipast: Varied appetizers, hors d'oeuvres.

back-friend: A secret enemy.

bagnio: A brothel; also, a bathhouse.

bantling: A young child, esp. a bastard.

bays: The laurel wreath for excellence.

bed: A bed or a dining couch.

blade of rue: A clump of herbs.

bugger: One guilty of unnatural vice, a low wretch.

capon: A eunuch; also, a catamite (*which see*).

carman: A gladiator in a chariot.

carted: Conveyed publicly in a cart as a punishment.

catamite: A boy used by a man in pederasty.

chapman: A merchant, trader.

chaps: Jaws.

close-stool: A stool or box to hold a chamber pot.

coll: To embrace, hug.

collop: A slice of meat.

comrogue: A fellow rogue.

costive: Constipated.

creepmouse, play at: Engage in furtive sexual play.

cuirassier: An armed man.

cullion: A base fellow.

dead lift: A situation taxing one's utmost powers.

denarius: A Roman silver coin.

downright Dunstable: Completely tipsy.

fardel: A burden.

Ganymede: The beautiful youth taken by Jupiter to be cupbearer to the gods; thus, a euphemism for a catamite (*which see*).

garnish-money: Money given as a fee.

green, vile: Trimalchio's servant wears green, one of the four colors—blue, green, white, and red—of competitors in the circus.

groat: A fourpenny piece.

hanging-sleeves: A child's garment.

house-of-office: A toilet.

Hummums: A famous bathhouse in Covent Garden, London.

iron garters: Fetters.

itch: A venereal disease.

Jack-Pudding: A buffoon, merry andrew.

jakes: Dirtiness, excrement.

Littleton: A noted English jurist (1407?-1481).

make-bate: A person who excites quarrels.

make-game: An object of ridicule, butt.

man of Gotham: A wiseacre, simpleton.

manchet: A piece of white bread.

maze: A state of bewilderment.

mewed up: Confined.

metheglin: A spiced drink; mead.

Opimian: Of Opimius' vintage (Opimius was consul in 121 B.C., an extraordinary year for wines).

pathic: A catamite (*which see*).

pett: A fit of anger.

plat: A flat surface.

process: A lawsuit.

pye at his bolster: Lit., "a magpie at his sofa"; a nagging or henpecking wife.

restiness: Inertia, sluggishness.

roister: A reveler.

rubb: An obstacle, difficulty.

runagate: A vagabond.

sapless: Lacking vitality.

Sevirs' Lodge: A Sevir Augustalis was an official responsible for carrying out the worship of the Emperor; one of his privileges was to sit on a throne.

slocked: Lured.

slubber-slops: A slovenly person.

splatchy: Blotchy.

steep: A hill.

tertian ague: A fever of a malarial character, occurring intermittently.

trapaned: Lured, snared.

washy: Weak, lacking vigor.